4/03

THE THREE SONS OF ADAM JONES

Old Adam Jones showed his sons no love, no mercy. All he wanted from them was absolute obedience. Ruthless, domineering, fast with his guns, the hard-nosed old rancher hated two things more than anything else—back talk and women. Nobody talked back to Adam Jones—at least not for long—and no woman had set foot on the ranch for years.

Then Adam Jones went on a trip and all hell broke loose. Even Adam's women-hungry sons might have walked around the big trouble if they hadn't found a pretty girl lying half dead on the prairie. After that they were ready to kill the old man or anybody else who crossed them. And a lot of fast guns were willing to try.

THE THREE SONS OF ADAM JONES

Wayne D. Overholser

GUNSMOKE

This hardback edition 2003
by Chivers Press
by arrangement with
Golden West Literary Agency

Copyright © 1969 by Wayne D. Overholser.
All rights reserved.

ISBN 0 7540 8216 4

British Library Cataloguing in Publication Data available.

Printed and bound in Great Britain by
BOOKCRAFT, Midsomer Norton, Somerset

THE THREE SONS OF ADAM JONES

Chapter I

JUDY DUNN stared at Jim Turnbull's broad back as he rode directly in front of her and wished she had had a gun. If she did, she'd shoot him right between the shoulder blades. She hated him. God, how she hated him. She had not known what it was to really hate anyone until she had run away from home a month ago with Turnbull. She had thought home was bad, but it had been heaven compared to this.

The Kid rode behind her leading the pack horse. She was afraid of him although she knew she didn't have any reason to be. He was a big, strong boy who worshipped Turnbull and wanted to be the kind of man he was.

Judy guessed the boy was sixteen though it was hard to tell for sure. He wasn't quite right in the head, but he could do the simple camp chores that Turnbull wanted done, and when the gang held up a bank, the Kid could be depended on to hold the horses.

Judy glanced back at the boy who gave her his usual innocuous grin. She didn't hate him. He wasn't worth hating. Actually he had been good to her, doing some of the little things around camp that Turnbull never offered to do. She smiled back at the Kid and turned her head to stare at Turnbull's back again.

To him, the boy was no more than an animal who could be depended on to do what he was told. The sorry part of the whole stupid business was that she was in just about the same category as the Kid. When Turnbull was tired of her, he'd get rid of her, but he'd raise hell if she tried to walk out on him.

Sooner or later she was going to walk out. She'd do it this minute if she knew how to escape Turnbull's anger. At first she'd been afraid to leave him, having no money and riding through a strange and empty land as they had been doing. For some reason she wasn't afraid now. She had finally decided she would rather starve than go on this way, riding day after day, worn out, half sick, and never having a chance even to take a bath.

Turnbull had been glancing at the creek as he watched for a camp site. Now, reaching a clump of quakies, he said, "This'll do."

That was his way. He never asked her what she wanted. There had been times when they had camped near towns and she had said she wanted to spend the night in a hotel, to sleep in a bed and get cleaned up and buy some decent clothes. He'd always said no. It was cheaper to camp and cook their meals over a fire. He said he didn't want to show his face in town if he could help it. He was lying. He was too stingy to pay for her room and meals.

She learned not to argue. She accepted his orders and did everything she was asked to do, and all the time her hate for him grew steadily. If this was romantic love, she wanted none of it.

Somehow, some way, she'd escape. Maybe this would be the night. She had tried it only once, about a week ago when they'd been camped on the other side of the Continental Divide near the head of the Poudre. It had been just before dawn and she'd thought he was sound asleep. She had got up and cat-footed toward the horses, but Turnbull who slept very lightly called out, "Where you going?"

"I'm taking a walk," she answered tartly.

A moment later she returned to the fire, but she didn't sleep any more that night. To think she could saddle a horse and ride out of camp without Turnbull hearing her was crazy. She didn't know what she'd been thinking of, but she guessed a person who was desperate enough would try anything. She was still desperate, she told herself as she dismounted wearily, but next time she wouldn't try to get away until she thought of something that would work.

Turnbull took care of the horses while the Kid started a fire and cut enough wood to last the night. They had crossed the Rockies and had dropped to a lower elevation on the western slope, but they were still up high and it would be cold before morning.

Judy cooked supper. Turnbull hunkered beside the fire and ate. When he was done, he said to her, "I figure we're about five miles from Hillcrest. I'm riding down the creek to look it over. You two stay here till I get back. I'll be gone a day or two."

She sipped her coffee and nodded, saying nothing. There was nothing to say. She might have accepted his way of life if he had kept any of the promises he had made to her back in Kansas, but she knew now he had never intended to.

She gathered from Turnbull's talk that she was only one of several women who had left their homes to ride off with him. The others had been dropped when he tired of them or saw other women he liked better. She had no illusions about her future. She would go the same way.

He rolled a cigarette and lighted it. He said, "There's plenty of grub for you and the Kid. I'll fetch some back with me when I come. The rest of the outfit will be riding into Hillcrest in a few days and I want to be on hand when they show up. The county fair starts in a couple of weeks and that's when the big money rolls into town. There ain't a bank within fifty miles, so they leave their money in a store safe. It'll be an easy job, then we'll ride south to Mexico."

He patted his money belt, smiling his easy smile the way he had the first he'd seen her. "I figure we'll live like a king and queen when we get on the other side of the Rio Grande."

He was lying again. It was easier for him to lie than it was to tell the truth. Her gaze followed him as he walked toward the horses. She had not been with him during any of the holdups and she didn't want to be. She had seen only a few members of his gang and she didn't want to see the rest of them.

Once, several outlaws had showed up when they were

7

camped on the South Platte near Fort Morgan. They had considered hitting a bank there, but gave it up because it was too small to be worth the effort.

Later some of the outfit had ridden into their camp on the Poudre after they'd left Fort Collins. That must have been when they had worked out the plan for robbing the store in Hillcrest. She had not learned exactly how they operated, but apparently the outlaws met and robbed a bank or store or stagecoach, then disbanded to meet somewhere else. If the law caught up with them, it would never get more than the two or three who happened to be together at that particular time.

Turnbull saddled his black gelding, said something to the Kid, then mounted and rode south along the creek. Judy watched him until he was among the quakies downstream, then she began cleaning up. She had been left alone with the Kid before, but she had not been as desperate then as she was now. She didn't know where she was going or what she would do. All she knew was that she was going.

The night was a long one. She slept only in snatches, then she would wake and lay staring at the sky through the limbs and quivering leaves. The fire had died down, but the Kid was sleeping too soundly to build it up. It went out and she was cold, but she lay there, shivering and thinking about her future. She was in a ranch country. She was capable and she wasn't afraid of work. She'd find a job. She knew she would.

When it was daylight, she dressed. The Kid stirred and finally sat up. He said, "Want a fire?"

"Yes."

He pulled on his boots, then tipped his head back and looked at her. He said, "Jim figgers you're fixing to run off. You try it and I'll bust your purty little neck."

So Turnbull had read her mind. She didn't say anything to the Kid. No use arguing with him. If Turnbull had told him to break her neck that was exactly what he would do. Apparently Turnbull figured that the Kid's threat would be enough to keep her in camp.

She picked up the coffee pot to take it to the creek, thinking she would fill it, then she set it back on the ground. The Kid was starting to build a fire, his back to

8

her as he used his knife to slice off long, curling shavings of dry quakie wood.

What she did then was sheer impulse. She picked up a short length of quakie limb as big as her arm and, gripping it with both hands, brought it down across his head with all the strength she had. The blow jarred and hurt her; the sound was a strange, hollow *thwack* as if his head was as empty as she had thought. He toppled forward across the coals of the night's fire and lay still.

She dropped the quakie limb and ran to the horses, fighting the panic that swept over her. She had killed him. She had smashed his skull. She didn't stop to look, but she knew that was what she had done.

Quickly she saddled her bay mare and mounted. She rode back along the creek, remembering they had passed a road that was hardly more than a trail. It had crossed the creek and wound to the top of the mesa in switchbacks. It must lead to a ranch, she thought.

The only thing that mattered now was to go some place where Jim Turnbull would never find her. He would kill her, she knew, not only for running away but for what she had done to the Kid.

There was the law, too. If it caught up with her, she would hang for murder. She crossed the creek and started the climb through the scrub oak to the top of the mesa.

Chapter II

As soon as Adam Jones and his three sons finished dinner in the Hillcrest Hotel dining room, Adam scooted his chair back and belched a great, rumbling belch. "Time for me to get down to the train," he said. "I don't want my steers to get to Denver ahead of me."

He rose, a giant of a man, six feet three inches tall and weighing better than two hundred fifty pounds. No lard on him anywhere, just solid bone and hard muscle as all three of his boys had learned by experience.

His wife had run off with another man years ago, so Adam had been forced to raise his sons without the help of any woman. He had no need of one on the ranch, he said. Women were all right to sleep with when he went to town, but he didn't trust them and he didn't want one around. As far as the boys were concerned, he demanded instant obedience, and he received it.

He marched out of the dining room, the boys following. He stopped at the desk to pay for their meal, clapped his Stetson on his head and stalked out through the street door and down the slope to the tracks. Bud, the youngest of the sons, grinned as he looked past Dolan, the middle boy, and Luke, the oldest, to his father's huge, proud body, and had to struggle to hold his laughter back.

Bud knew well enough he had better hold it back. Laughter was one thing Adam couldn't stand. There had been very little laughter on the Big J as long as Bud could remember. He had a very hazy recollection of his mother who had been a slim, attractive woman, a kind of a flibbertigibbet, Luke always said.

Luke was three years older than Bud, so he remembered their mother better than either of his brothers. Bud had lost his memory picture entirely, but he did remember the bright, happy tone of her laughter and the songs she taught them as she put them to bed. After she left the Big J, there was no laughter all, and no singing.

What amused Bud was the way they always lined out just as they were doing now, his father in front, then Luke who was almost as big as Adam, Dolan who was kind of a misfit with his tall, gangling body and near-sighted eyes and thick-lensed glasses, and finally Bud in the rear. It was like a herd of bulls, with the big papa bull in front and the three little bulls trailing behind. There was no room for cows in this herd.

When they reached the caboose, the engine at the other end of the cattle train was snorting and pawing ready to go. Adam said, "I'll be gone a week, maybe less if I get tired of the big city." He turned to the caboose and then swung back. "Don't let no women come on the Big J while I'm gone. You hear?"

"We won't, Pa," Luke promised. "If a woman chases any of us, I'll scare her off."

Adam grinned. "Sure you will, boy. I know that, but I thought I'd better say it anyway. There's plenty of women around here who'd move in with you if they had the chance."

He swung up and disappeared inside the caboose. A moment later the train began to move. It gathered speed and rolled upstream toward the Rockies. Some time early tomorrow it would be over the top and heading downslope toward Denver.

The three of them stood motionless staring at the rear end of the caboose. Bud knew the thought that was in his mind was also singing through the heads of his brothers. They had talked enough about things to know all three felt the same way and all three were ashamed.

Bud couldn't keep from hoping that the train would go off the track and Adam would get killed. Or maybe he'd get into a row in Denver and somebody would shoot him. Sure, Bud was ashamed of his thoughts, but the fact remained that if something happened to Adam, it would turn night into day for Bud and his brothers.

Without a word, they walked back to the hotel and went into the bar. Adam ran a bill here. The boys didn't drink because they had no money. They worked for their keep and had all their lives. Adam said they were too young to drink. They knew it could go on that way the rest of their lives if they let it, but they also knew it wouldn't.

Luke was twenty-four, Dolan was twenty-two, and in less than a week, Bud would be twenty-one. They'd be free to ride out then. They owned nothing but the guns they carried in their holsters, their clothes, their saddles, and their horses. Not much to pay for the hard work and long hours they'd put into making the Big J the best spread in the county.

They bellied up to the bar as Luke said, "Whisky."

The bartender looked them over and said, "You boys are too young to drink."

"Whisky," Dolan said. "You're getting hard of hearing, Jumbo."

The fat bartender shook his head. "No, I ain't hard of hearing, but I know what your pa says. He was plumb ringy about his bill last year when he got back from Denver and came in to pay up. He claimed I'd made a mistake, and if there's anybody in the county I don't want to tangle with, it's your pa."

"We've had this argument before," Luke said, placing his big hands palm down on the cherrywood bar. "We ain't fixing to argue about it today. I don't care how you fool Pa about his bill, but you're serving us whisky or I'm coming across the bar and I'll beat your damn brains out."

"What's more, I'll bust every bottle you've got," Bud added, easing his gun out of leather and sliding the barrel over the edge of the bar. "I'll start with that old Crow . . ."

"By God, I believe you'd do it," the bartender said, staring at Bud.

He wasn't scared of Luke who was as big as he was, and he wasn't scared of Dolan who'd never had a fight in his life, but Bud buffaloed him. Bud was the runt of the

12

family, five feet nine and just under one hundred fifty pounds, but he had freckles and red hair and a jaw like an English bull dog, and he'd taken more lickings from his dad than Luke and Dolan put together.

"You know I would," Bud said.

Luke laughed. He was inordinately fond of his little brother. The three of them had always got along, sometimes lying to protect each other from their father's anger, with Luke and Bud taking the blame for Dolan's mistakes.

Dolan had a talent for doing the wrong thing. He was cut out for something besides being a cowboy. He hadn't found out what it was, but if he'd been allowed to go to school, he would have. Luke and Ben had often talked about it when Dolan wasn't with them. They had promised themselves that somehow they were going to see that Dolan had his chance, but they couldn't do it as long as they slaved on the Big J.

The bartender scratched an ear and finally shrugged. He set three glasses and a bottle on the bar and walked to the other end, shaking his head and talking to himself. Luke poured the drinks and said, "Little Brother, I wish I could scare folks the way you do."

Bud laughed and downed his drink and said, "You're just a big, good-natured bear. Everybody loves you and you can't scare people who love you."

Luke snorted. "Hell, I wish I knew how to make 'em hate me. You don't get nowhere on the Big J with love."

"Oh, I don't know about that." Dolan turned the glass in his fingers, staring at the amber liquid. He had no taste for whisky, but he had come along just to be with Luke and Bud. "If we had a woman . . ."

"A woman," Bud jeered. "You ain't tasted your drink, but you've addled your brain just looking at it. Or maybe it's the fumes. You expect to find a woman in the brush?"

"Maybe," Dolan said. "You find surprising things in the brush sometimes. All I know is that a woman could sure change a lot of things at home."

"I know something else," Luke said. "We ain't waiting for no woman to show up. We're changing things ourselves. The day Bud's twenty-one, we're asking Pa for our wages from the time we was twenty-one and then we're riding out. He's had the cheapest crew he'll ever have working for him. It's past time we was moving on."

"What'll he get for the critters this time?" Dolan asked.

"Five thousand, maybe more," Luke said. "He's got ten thousand hidden around the house somewhere. He can afford to pay us and then go out and hire hisself a crew."

"You gonna have the guts to face him?" Bud asked.

Luke took his second drink and turned to look at Bud. "I don't know," he said slowly. "I wish I did. Right now I think I have, but I don't know. When I face that old he-coon and he bellers at me a time or two, I just naturally start to wilt."

"He'll come back feeling like a soretailed grizzly," Bud said. "He'll spend a week in Denver trying to outdrink, outfight, outcuss and outscrew every other cowman in Denver. He'll be ready to murder us if we jump him right off."

"I know," Luke said. "Sometimes I figger I must have been born a coward as far as pa is concerned."

For a moment they stood there in silence, all three burdened by the sure knowledge that they could buck anybody and anything in the world except Adam Jones. Bud figured he could if the others backed him all the way, but he didn't have any faith in either brother, on that score.

"Let's ride," Luke said.

They turned from the bar and strode back to the loading chutes where they had left their horses. Mounting, they took the Banner Creek road for five miles, then turned east to climb to the mesa. Here the flat grassland with a sprinkling of sage stretched out in front of them for miles, broken here and there by a steep-banked arroyo. They stopped to blow their horses, the Big J buildings visible to the north.

"We could have a good deal here," Luke said thoughtfully. "We deserve it, but Pa would never give it to us."

"He wouldn't give us the time of day," Dolan said resentfully.

14

Bud glanced at him, understanding the resentment. Adam Jones savvied his middle son the least of the three. To him it was a waste of time to read a book or go to school or try to write something for the Hillcrest Weekly Herald the way Dolan did. It was womanly to go to church once in a while which Dolan had done when he was younger. Adam seldom beat him. He just cut him down with his tongue. Bud knew this hurt Dolan worse than the beatings Adam gave him and Luke.

"Let's git to moving," Bud said. "Damn it, we oughta ride out today and let the outfit go to hell."

They rode on, all three knowing they wouldn't and none of them really sure they'd do it even after Adam got home. Dark clouds were rolling up along the peaks to the east and thunder began to follow the jagged lightning thrusts. A gullywasher was on the way and they touched up their horses to beat the storm home.

A mile farther on Bud saw something beside the small stream that drained the mesa. He didn't know what it was. Just a flash of color in the tall grass, but it didn't belong there. He swung off the road, calling, "Come here, both of you."

They turned back, irritated by the delay, then reined up beside Bud, staring bug-eyed.

"My God," Luke said. "A woman!"

15

Chapter III

IT WAS a woman, all right, a young one. She'd even be a pretty one if she were cleaned up and had a decent dress. She must, Bud thought, have been on the road for a long time, as dirty as she was and with her riding skirt torn in half a dozen places.

She lay on her back, a strand of dark brown hair falling across her pale face. For a moment Bud thought she was dead. He dismounted and felt of her pulse. It was, strong and regular, so she was a long ways from being dead. She had fainted or had been knocked cold. Maybe she had been bucked off a horse. Carefully he ran his fingers over her head and found a sizeable lump.

Bud stood up and faced his brothers who were staring at the woman, as motionless as if they were frozen in their saddles. He said, "See a horse anywhere around here?"

His question jarred them out of their trance. Luke stood up in his stirrups and looked around. He said, "Yeah, there's a horse yonder in that little gully. A bay."

"He must have got boogered by something and dumped her," Bud said. "She sure is plumb out of it." He looked at Dolan and grinned. "Just like you said. You never know what you're gonna find in the brush. I never figured we'd find a woman, but we did."

"What are we gonna do with her?" Luke demanded.

"Yeah, what are we going to do with her?" Dolan asked. "We can't take her home."

"Why not?" Bud asked. "Looks to me like it's the

16

one time we can take her home. We'll keep her for a week till pa gets home. By that time maybe we'll like her well enough to go on keeping her."

"My God, have you been nibbling on loco weed?" Luke asked. "Pa would kill us and her, too."

Dolan nodded agreement. "He'd go clear out of his head. We can take her home now, but we'd better get her out of the house before pa shows up."

Bud ran his sweaty hands across the front of his shirt. He looked up at the storm-black sky with its flashes of lightning, laughing shakily. He was thinking that if his father found the girl in the house when he came home, his performance would make all this disturbance in the sky look like a small boy's celebration of the Fourth of July.

"We don't know nothing about her," he said slowly. "She may turn out to be some floozy who couldn't stand the whorehouse no longer. Maybe she stole a horse and started riding. I figured we'll soon find out, and that if she's a decent woman, we'd better keep her. It's like Dolan said a while ago, a woman could change a lot of things at home. I think it would be a good thing to have her in the house when pa walks through the door. What'll happen if he slaps her around?"

"I savvy what you're getting at," Luke said sourly. "If we start liking her purty well, I guess that's all it would take to put some starch into our backbones. I kind of like to think we could handle pa if all three of us tackled him at the same time."

"I might even shoot him," Bud said. "I hate him enough to do it and I've sure got plenty of reason. I've never really stood up to him on anything that was important, but if he lays a hand on her, I think I could."

"Pick her up and let's take her home," Dolan said. "We're going to get wet if we don't get a move on."

Bud climbed into the saddle. "Hand her up to me, Luke. I'll carry her in. Or I'll hand her up to you if you want to tote her home."

"I'll get her," Luke said, and swung down.

He bent over the girl and started to slip his hands under her shoulders and knees, then froze. He moistened his lips

17

and glanced up at Bud easily. "I ain't never touched a woman before," he said.

"You're going to," Bud said, "right now."

Slowly Luke began to move again. Bud, watching, thought he went at it about the way a man would ease away from a rattlesnake. He slid one arm under her legs and another under her shoulders and lifted her, still moving in that slow, deliberate way. When he had her clear of the ground, he suddenly wheeled toward Bud and shoved the girl into his brother's arms.

"You can have her," he said as if he had trouble breathing. "Maybe pa's right about women."

"Hell, she won't bite you," Bud said. "No, pa's dead wrong. It's just that we ain't never been around 'em, and I guess a man's just naturally scared of anything he don't know about." He held her soft body in front of him, liking the feel of it. "We need to find out something about women, and maybe this is our chance. Come on."

He wasn't holding her right, but he didn't know how he could do any better. She was like a sack of wool. Her legs dangled on one side of him and her head rolled around on the other, but she was unconscious, so she didn't know how uncomfortable she was.

Luke and Dolan rode ahead of him, both glancing back now and then. Dolan was leading the girl's bay mare. They were scared, he thought, and he wasn't sure why it was any different with him. Maybe it was because he saw in her a chance to get at his father.

Again the prospect of having Adam Jones walk into the house and see a young woman there brought a soft laugh out of him, then the laughter faded. There would be nothing humorous about the scene that was bound to follow. He felt guilty then and decided they couldn't do it. They had no right to drag the girl through a dangerous situation as this was bound to be.

The storm clouds had completely covered the sky, so except for the moments when ragged tongues of lightning lashed the earth, the light was very thin by the time they reached the house. Bud said, "Get down and take her, Luke. Tote her inside. Better put her down on the couch. Pa's room is always a mess."

18

Luke dismounted and took the girl out of Bud's arms. He said, "You can carry her into the . . ."

"My left arm's gone to sleep," Bud said. "You bring her."

He stepped down and, running ahead of Luke and the girl, held the screen back, then shoved the door open. Dolan was leading the girl's bay toward the corral. Bud yelled, "Don't pull the saddle off Old Blue. I'm going back to town for the doc."

Luke stumbled into the front room and lurched across it to the black leather couch. He dumped the girl on it and stepped back. He said, "I'll go get the doc. I ain't staying here with a woman and Dolan. Hell, Dolan wouldn't be no help."

"I'm your little brother," Bud said. "I wouldn't be no help, neither."

Luke glowered at him. "For some reason which I don't savvy, you seem to take to women more'n Dolan or me. Maybe you've been getting chummy with some floozy in Hillcrest."

"It ain't my fault that I'm not," Bud snapped. "If Pa ever gave me two dollars, I would be. Go start a fire in the kitchen and fill the boiler with water. She's got to have a bath."

"What are you gonna do?" Luke demanded.

"I'm gonna get a blanket to put over her," Bud said, "and then I'm gonna fetch the doc. You and Dolan clean up pa's room. Then do some work in here." He glanced at the dirty floor and the dusty furniture and the pile of newspapers and magazines and catalogs that covered the claw-footed oak stand and shook his head. "Talk about a stinking boar's nest. This ain't no fit place for a woman and that's a fact."

"Now you wait a minute," Luke bellowed. "I'll give the orders. Like you said, you're my little brother. I'll ride to town. I'll fetch Doc Blake. You put the boiler of water on the stove. You clean up the damned house."

Bud ran into his father's bedroom and returned a moment later with a blanket which he spread over the motionless girl. He looked at Luke, chewing on his lower lip a moment, then he nodded. "All right, you go ahead, but there's one more thing you've got to do when you get to

19

town. We can't let her wear the duds she's got on and there sure ain't no female clothes around here, so you go to the store and buy everything a woman needs."

Luke's mouth sprung open. Then he wiped a hand across his face and groaned. "Now ain't you the cute one? What do I know about women's duds? Maybe you do, so go ahead."

"All right, I will," Bud said, and left the house.

Dolan was on his way back to get Luke's horse when Bud reached Old Blue. He said, "You help Luke clean the house up. We'll put her in Pa's room if you can get it cleaned up so it's halfway decent. She's got to have a bath, so I told Luke to heat a boiler of water."

"Bath?" Dolan was horrified. "We can't take her clothes off and give her a bath."

"Maybe she'll be able to do it," Bud said, "but shes gonna have one if we have to give it to her."

He untied his slicker and slipped it on, glancing up at the sky as he swung into the saddle. The storm was close now. At least they had reached the house before it hit and the girl was dry. As sick and tired as she must be, a soaking would have given her a chill that likely would end up in mountain fever.

He wondered about that blow on the head. He had heard of people being unconscious for days and knew they'd have to take the girl to town if she didn't come out of it. Doc Blake could tell them what to do. It was going to be awkward and gossip was bound to follow if they kept the girl, but he hoped they could.

The storm hit while he was still on the mesa with the violence that was typical of summer rains in this country. It moved across the flat grassland in a silver curtain, a gullywasher that threatened to flatten everything, and then in an incredibly short time, it was gone, leaving behind a drowned world.

Bud rode down the slope to Banner Creek, a stream of muddy water cutting a channel in the trail. By the time he reached the valley, the wet earth was steaming. The sun came out and burned Bud's back. The air was still heavy and damp, and the tangy smell of sage and pine filled Bud's nostrils. This heady fragrance always followed a summer storm and Bud enjoyed it. He had never lived anywhere else and he knew this damp, scented air was something he would miss if and when he left the country.

He turned south when he reached Banner Creek, touching Old Blue up because it would be well after dark before he could get back to the Big J. He saw a horse tied between the road and the creek. A kid was trying to get a fire started. That, Bud thought, would be quite a trick after the storm.

He wondered who the boy was and why he was here. Maybe some older man was with him. Maybe the man had gone to town for supplies. Then he shrugged. It wasn't any of his business. It wasn't unusual for a boy in his middle teens to ride through the country looking for work. Maybe he had run away from home.

He'd tell the sheriff when he got to Hillcrest. The law man might want to ask about the horse. The chances were good it had been stolen. He rode on downstream, Old Blue slipping in the mud so it was impossible to make good time.

The sun was almost down when he rode into Hillcrest. He went directly to the doctor's house, hoping the medico wasn't out on a call. He forgot all about the boy who was camped up the creek.

Chapter IV

JIM TURNBULL had left his horse in a livery stable and gone directly to the hotel when he had reached town the previous evening. He was tired and a little nervous about the job they had planned. He wasn't sure why, except that he often felt this way when he rode into a town in which they had planned to pull a robbery.

None of his men would be here yet, but they'd straggle in within the next week. Strangers were expected in Hillcrest with the fair only two weeks away. It was unlikely that they would attract any unfavorable attention and that, of course, was the way they wanted it. After they had cleaned the store safe out, they'd scatter and the sheriff would have no idea where they had gone.

For a time he stood by the window looking down into the street. Hillcrest was like a hundred other little cowtowns Turnbull had seen, a single business block on a bench above the river, the buildings all on the north side of the street. Just beyond the street the slope tipped down to the railroad tracks. The river was on the south side of the rails.

A freight train rumbled by as Turnbull stood there, its whistle cutting into the night air. It rolled on downstream toward Grand Junction, not even slowing up as it roared through Hillcrest. Turnbull doubted that three hundred people lived here, but for the two days of the fair there would be thousands. The business men would make as much money in these two days as they did the other three hundred sixty-three.

22

Turnbull rolled and lighted a cigarette, thinking that the business men had taken a big risk years ago when they had set out to make the Hillcrest Fair the biggest racing event on the western slope and had put up cash prizes which were fabulous. The risk had paid off. Now people came from Craig and Steamboat Springs in the north to Durango in the south, from the Continental Divide on the east to Utah on the west.

He had never been here before, but he had heard about it for years, particularly the enormous amount of money that changed hands during these two days. Even discounting the stories as being exaggerated, it would still be enough to give everyone in the outfit a good chunk of dinero.

He slept late, not going down to breakfast until the middle of the morning. He ordered ham and eggs and coffee, watching the blonde waitress walk away from him toward the kitchen door with a neat wiggle of hips and butt. He would have to encourage her, he thought, although for the time being Judy was all he wanted.

When the waitress returned with his plate and cup of coffee, he said, "I hear the fair is a big event in this country."

"Oh yes," she said, smiling. "It's the biggest event anywhere around."

"Anybody in town for it yet?" he asked.

"A few," she answered. "We won't get the big rush until next week. The men who are entering horses in the races always get here ahead of the main crowd."

"The hotel can't put everybody up, can it?"

"Goodness, no," she said. "We don't even try. Most people camp. They'll be all up and down the river and some will even go up Banner Creek. It's a crowd, I tell you."

She smiled again and left him. Yes, he'd certainly have to encourage her. He would have to establish some kind of identity as he always did when he went into a new town. Usually he passed himself off as a cattle buyer or a man looking for a place to settle down. He decided the latter would be the best bet in this situation. Cattle were raised around here, right, but with the fair attracting more people every year, he judged there would be more interest in

23

horses than cattle, so maybe he'd better look for a horse ranch.

He left the dining room as soon as he finished breakfast and moved along the boardwalk on the north side of the street. There was just the one general store, Runkel's Mercantile, but he didn't go in. Beyond the store was the Palace Saloon, then a jewelry store, Cassidy's Bar, a drug store, and a hardware store. The blacksmith shop was the last business building. On beyond were a dozen or more houses.

Turning back, he stepped into Cassidy's Bar and ordered whisky. He asked, "You know of any ranches for sale? This country looks good to me. I've got a notion I'd like to settle down here."

"Sure," the bartender said. "There's plenty of ranches for sale if you've got the price."

"I've got it, all right," Turnbull said. "I've been raising horses out of Fort Morgan a piece and sold out a month or more ago. I figured I'd move to Denver and be a town dude." He shook his head and grinned. "Hell, I soon found out that wasn't no life for me."

"You'll like it here," the bartender said. "We've got the most salubrious climate in the state of Colorado. I'll tell you who to see. A feller name of Max Early sells real estate. He's got an office between the hotel and the livery stable."

"I'll look him up," Turnbull said and left the saloon.

He idled away the rest of the morning walking around town and along the tracks and even had a look at the fair grounds. There were a few small buildings that were probably used to show the fresh vegetable and fruit and canning and sewing and whatnots that people love to exhibit, and a couple of barns for the livestock, but it was plain that the races were the most important function of the fair.

An old man was cutting weeds along the track in front of the grandstand. He said, "Howdy" and Turnbull said, "They tell me that a man can get as big a bet as he wants during the fair."

The old man stopped mowing and, dropping the scythe he had been using, he wiped his face with his bandanna. "He sure as hell can. I don't know how much money

24

you've got, but I can tell you that if you ain't a millionaire, you'll find plenty of men who'll cover every nickel you want to put up."

Turnbull laughed. "I ain't a millionaire, but I've got some money. I aim to be around here for a spell. I'm looking for a horse ranch. You know of any for sale?"

"Plenty of good ranches in this country," the old man said. "You can find what you want if you can pay for it."

"Maybe I'd better find a spread and pay for it before the races," Turnbull said.

The old man nodded. "I've saw plenty of fellers lose their spreads and their shirts," he said as he offered his hand. "I'm Monte Mullins. I was purty well fixed once myself, but I lost everything I had right here on this track a couple of years ago. Now I'm glad to get a job like this."

"Glad to know you, Monte," Turnbull said, shaking the old man's hand. "I'm Jim Turnbull. I'll buy you a drink the next time I see you in Cassidy's."

"I'll remind you of that," Mullins said.

"How much dinero do you suppose changes hands a day?" Turnbull asked. "I mean, during the fair?"

"A hundred thousand," Mullins answered. "Maybe more. Most of it's locked up in the store safe through the day. Every afternoon when the races are over, Abe Runkel opens the safe and hands out the dinero and the men pay off their bets. You never seen such a pile of greenbacks and gold as Abe hauls out of there."

"Looks like somebody would start a bank here in Hillcrest," Turnbull said.

Mullins shrugged. "Naw. Just the two big days in this town, and the rest of the time it's so dead it stinks. Nobody could make anything out of a bank in this burg. Abe, he don't mind taking care of the dinero. He says for two days he feels like a rich man with all that dinero in his safe."

"Ever been held up or robbed?"

Mullins snorted. "Never has. I feel sorry for the gent who tries it. We get some mighty tough hands in here. I reckon a few of 'em are outlaws, all right, but most folks

25

come here for the racing and the betting, and it would sure go hard on anybody who tackled it."

"I'll be moseying back to the hotel and get my dinner," Turnbull said. "Don't forget that drink."

"I don't aim to," Mullins said. "It ain't often I get a drink no more. Can't afford it on what I make doing odd jobs like this."

Walking back to the hotel, Turnbull told himself that Monte Mullins, like all old men, were bound to tell a good story. Still, if you cut one hundred thousand dollars in half, you'd still have a sizeable chunk of dinero.

He ate dinner, then took his horse from the livery stable and rode up the river for several miles. Returning to town, he rode downriver. When he came back to the hotel for supper, it was late afternoon and a storm was moving down from the high peaks to the east.

As soon as he finished eating, he went into the store and bought coffee, bacon, and beans. Abe Runkel was a little man with dark, beady eyes and the eager air of one who doesn't want to lose a sale. The safe was in the rear of the long room, a big safe, but that didn't worry Turnbull. One of his men, Cold Dam Summers, could open any safe. At least he had never found one he couldn't open.

Turnbull didn't try to get close to the safe. There'd be plenty of time for that later. He shook hands with Runkel, gave the storekeeper his name, and said he was looking for a horse ranch. Runkel moved up close to him, looked around furtively, and said, "I've got just the place for you. It's across the river and up French Creek. I'll show you where it is any day you've got time to go."

"Thanks, Mr. Runkel," Turnbull said. "I'll take you up on that before long."

He left the store and tied the sack behind the saddle. He put his slicker on, knowing that the storm was close, but he didn't want Judy and the Kid to run out of grub. He decided he'd better ride to camp and see how they made out all day.

Judy hadn't said anything about leaving him, but he knew she was thinking of it. That had been plain enough for several days. He had never let a woman leave him and he wasn't starting with Judy. It was a matter of pride with

26

him what when it was time to separate from a woman, he did the separating.

He had barely left town when the storm hit. He turned his horse into a close-growing bunch of pines and sat his saddle, waiting for the rain to let up. It wasn't much protection, but it was better than staying in the open. For some reason he felt his nervousness growing and that wasn't the way it should go.

He couldn't remember feeling this way for so long. Usually his nervousness left as soon as he began exploring a town and talking to people. Maybe it was the booming thunder and the lightning that was bounding all around him. He never had been comfortable when he'd been caught in a thunderstorm. Finally he decided it was Judy. Maybe he'd better work her over a little just to show her he wasn't tired of her yet.

He went on as soon as the storm eased up. He saw a rider ahead of him and reined off the road into the willows along the creek and waited until the man went by. He was a young cowboy, probably from some ranch up the creek.

Turnbull rode on as soon as the man was out of sight. When he reached the camp where he had left Judy and the Kid, he saw the boy hunched over a smoky fire. The girl wasn't in sight. Turnbull untied the sack of grub and tossed it on the ground as the Kid straightened up and walked toward him.

"Sure glad you got here, Mr. Turnbull," he said. "I can't get a good fire going after that rain. It just smolders. I ain't cooked supper yet and looks like I ain't going to. I thought I could ride into town with you and you could buy me a hot supper."

"You've got plenty of grub now." Turnbull motioned to the sack he had dropped. "Where's Judy?"

The Kid swallowed and looked past Turnbull at the side of the mountain west of the valley. "I don't know where she is," he said.

Something stirred in Turnbull, a yeasty kind of fear that was a new feeling for him. "What do you mean?" he asked roughly. "You don't know where she is?"

"I don't, Mr. Turnbull." The Kid swallowed. "Honest, I don't. We got up like usual this morning. I was gonna

27

build a fire for her, but before I could do it, she picked up a club and hit me over the head. I was sick when I woke up. My head's been hurting me ever since."

"What happened to Judy?" Turnbull grabbed the boy by the shoulders and shook him. "What in the hell happened to her?"

"She was gone," the boy answered. "I told you I didn't know what happened to her."

"You didn't go after her?"

"How could I?" the kid asked. "I said I didn't know where she went."

Turnbull slapped him on the face, a hard, head-rocking blow. "You damned fool!" he shouted. "You brainless whelp! I don't know why I left you with her. You'll never do it again."

He stepped back and drew his gun. The Kid's face turned pale when he realized what Turnbull intended to do. "No," he screamed. "Please, Mr. Turnbull. I've worked hard for you. You ain't got no call to shoot me. I told you it wasn't my fault. She hit me on the head with a club . . ."

Turnbull shot him, then shot him again as he was falling. After he was sprawled on the ground, Turnbull shot him three more times. He reloaded and holstered his gun. He picked up the sack of food and threw it into the willows on the other side of the creek, steadily cursing in an angry voice. He untied the Kid's horse and gave him a slap on the rump, then mounted and rode back to town.

Judy had left him. He couldn't put the thought out of his mind. It was a blow to his pride. He'd find her and bring her back. She couldn't go far. She didn't have any money. She'd have to find some place to stay and it would probably be on a ranch. He couldn't track after the storm. He'd just have to ride and look and ask some questions.

Then, when he was almost back to town, another thought came to him. Suppose she told everything she knew about him? She wouldn't, he assured himself. She was too scared of him. He'd told her plenty of times what would happen to her if she ever left him and talked.

But she had left him! Maybe she wasn't as scared of him as she'd let on. Maybe she would talk. By God, he had to find her and shut her mouth for good.

28

Chapter V

JUDY DUNN had no idea where she was when she came to. She couldn't even remember who she was or what had happened. She couldn't think because of the hammering in her head. It was dark, but a finger of lamplight fell into the room through the open door.

She heard men's voices speaking in a low tone, and she was aware that her blouse was torn, that her hair was disheveled, and when she put a hand to her head, she discovered a lump that hurt when she touched it.

For a time she lay motionless staring at the dark ceiling. She was on some sort of couch. If she knew even her name! Maybe she had done something terrible, had committed some crime and was running away. She tried to sit up, but her head threatened to split open, so she lay back immediately, gritting her teeth to keep from groaning.

Maybe these men would know who she was. What would she do if they didn't? Suddenly panic possessed her and she had to fight an impulse to scream. She put a hand on her forehead and tried to think, but her mind was a blank. Nothing came.

Two men appeared from the bedroom. She guessed it was a bedroom. At least they came through the door that had been open, the one in front carrying a lamp. He set it on a stand and both of them turned to her. She asked. "Who am I?"

They stared at her as if they could not believe what they had just heard her say. One was a big man, tall and broad-shouldered, the other almost as tall, but very skinny. He wore thick-lensed glasses. Both seemed scared, but the thin one was the worst. He was very nervous and fidgety, looking as if he were ready to take off in a dead run as soon as he found an excuse.

Finally the big man said, "We don't know who you are, ma'am. We was riding back from town when we found you purty close to the house. You was lying on the ground beside the creek. Looked like you'd been bucked off your mare. We fetched her home with us. She's a good-looking bay."

Judy looked at the big man, then at the skinny one. They were young, probably in their early twenties. They looked like good men, she thought. They weren't going to hurt her. How did she know that? She realized she didn't. She didn't know anything except that her head hurt.

She blurted, "You won't hurt me, will you?"

The question startled them. They looked at each other uneasily, then the big one said, "No, ma'am. We wouldn't hurt you no matter what. I'm Luke Jones. This is my brother Dolan. We've got a younger brother named Bud, but he ain't here. He went to town to get the doc for you." He cleared his throat, and asked as he shuffled his feet nervously, "You can't remember nothing?"

"Not a thing." She rubbed her forehead. "I seem to remember that I had done something terrible I shouldn't and I was trying to get away. I don't have anywhere to go, Mr. Jones. I'm scared. What will I do?"

"First you're going to have a bath," Luke said. "We've got a boiler of hot water on the kitchen stove and the tub's in the bedroom yonder. It ain't a very good room for you. It belongs to pa. He's gone to Denver with a shipment of steers and won't be back till the end of the week, so you can stay in his room. In the morning after a good sleep maybe you'll remember."

"Maybe I will;" she said.

"Don't worry about not having a place to go," Luke said. "Or being scared. You can stay here till you feel good and remember who you are. We won't let nobody hurt you. We don't have no woman on the place, so we don't have no woman's duds for you to wear, but Bud's kind of little, so we put a pair of his pants and one of his

30

shirts on the bed. After you take a bath, you put them on and then you get into bed and you stay there."

"All right," she said.

She knew she couldn't think for herself, so they had to do her thinking for her. If she could only remember who she was and why she was here and what she had been running away from.

"Are you hungry?" Luke asked.

"No," she answered. "I couldn't eat anything."

"We'll fetch the hot water," Luke said. "Then you go take a bath."

They left the room and returned a moment later, carrying a steaming boiler of water. They went on into the bedroom and she heard them pouring and talking and pouring some more, then they came back, Dolan carrying the empty boiler.

"Can you walk?" Luke asked.

She sat up and shut her eyes, the hammering pain in her head so bad she thought she was going to faint. She stayed upright until the worst of the pain passed, then she got to her feet. The room started to spin and she toppled forward. She would have fallen on her face if Luke hadn't caught her by an arm and steadied her.

He held her up until the world stopped whirling, and walked beside her into the bedroom, keeping his grip on her arm. She was uncertain of her footing, but she made it into the bedroom and sat down on the edge of the bed, her head in her hands.

Luke pulled her boots off, then he asked, "You want us to undress you?"

For the first time since she had regained consciousness, she felt like smiling. From the hesitant way Luke said it, she suspected that he was afraid she would say yes. "No," she said, "I can manage."

"You holler when you get into bed," he said.

She nodded. "All right."

They left the room, pulling the door shut behind them. Dolan had left a lamp on the bureau. She undressed slowly, then felt the water in the tub. It was warm, but not hot enough to be uncomfortable. She eased into it, holding to the edge of the bed.

She found that she was able to sit in the tub and keep

31

her feet in the water, and then she saw to her dismay that she was dirty. She was worse than dirty. She was filthy. No wonder these men knew she needed a bath.

She saw a bar of soap on a chair beside her. She picked it up and smelled of it and put it back. She couldn't use it. Maybe the men could, but it was laundry soap and would take her hide off. She scrubbed herself the best she could and discovered that the violent pounding in her head had diminished. She began to relax, wishing she had a mirror, but there wasn't one in the room.

She stayed in the water until it was almost cold, then she got out and, hanging to the back of the chair, dried herself with a towel they had left for her. She put the pants and shirt on and got into bed. The night was warm, the air heavy with moisture, so she had no need of pulling the covers over her. She stayed on top and was asleep in a matter of seconds.

Later she woke when Luke knocked on her door. She called sleepily, "Come in." Luke opened the door and stepped into the room, Dolan behind him. They carried the tub of water out, then Luke returned and picked up her clothes. For a moment he stood looking down at her. She thought he seemed ill at ease, perhaps made uncomfortable by having a woman in the house.

"You forgot to holler when you got into bed," he said.

"I'm sorry," she said. "I went right to sleep."

"Can I get anything for you?"

"No," she answered.

"You sleep as long as you want to in the morning," he said. "I think you'd better call one of us before you get up. We don't want you fainting and falling down."

"I'll see how I feel," she said.

He blew the lamp out and left the room, then she realized she had not heard the skinny one, Dolan, say a word. She wasn't so sleepy now, but lay on her back and stared at the dark ceiling, wondering if her memory would ever come back.

A terrible fear was nagging her now because she felt as if the door to her past was just about to open. She had a feeling she really did not want it to open. When it did, she would remember that she had killed a man, but where and when and why and who?

She had no answer for any of those questions, and she still didn't have them when she finally slid off into a deep and dreamless sleep.

Chapter VI

BUD JONES yanked on the bell pull of Dr. Blake's home and waited anxiously. When he did not get any response, he yanked again, his anxiety growing. He was afraid the medico was out of town on a call. Dr. Blake was an old man who had served the community most of his life, but he was still healthy and incredibly strong for a man his age and he had said repeatedly he had no intention of retiring.

This time Bud heard someone coming. The front door opened and the doctor stood there peering at Bud in the thinning light. He was still chewing on a bite of supper and was plainly out of sorts at being called away from his meal. He was tall and thin and stood as straight as a man half his age. Even with his white hair and white goatee and mustache, he had lost none of his professional bearing.

"Well, boy," Blake said, "what's on your mind?"

"You've got to harness up and come out to the Big J," Bud said. "We've got a young woman who fell off her horse, I guess. She was unconscious when I left home, so she couldn't tell us what had happened, but that's the way it looked."

"You think I'm going to harness up and drive seven or eight miles to see a woman who fell off a horse?" the doctor said testily. "Well, let me tell you something, young man. I don't have to do anything of the kind. I've got a baby coming and I'll be up all night, and I am not leaving town."

"We don't know what to do," Bud said. "We took her home and I laid her on the couch. She ain't moving or talking or doing anything." He swallowed, and asked. "What can we do? We don't know nothing about women, Doc."

"I never saw a man who did," Blake said, "but with your dad being half crazy hating women the way he is, I reckon you've had less chance to find out about them than the average man." He pulled at his goatee, studying Bud and smiling a little. "What do you think will happen when Adam gets home?"

"There'll be hell to pay," Bud said, "but we've made up our minds that we're leaving home, so it don't make no difference what he says or does. I'll be twenty-one by the time he gets back. I'm free to go, and Luke and Dolan are gonna ask him for wages, seeing as they've both worked for nothing ever since they were twenty-one. We'll likely take the girl with us unless she's got some place to go, but she's a stranger, so I figure she's lost."

The half-smile left the doctor's lips. He said gravely, "I guess you boys know your pa better'n I do, but I've seen what happens when somebody crosses him. He's damned near killed a couple of men with his hands because of some row that didn't amount to a hill of beans. I know because I patched those fellows up. You boys won't be no match for him."

"I guess we wouldn't be if we tackled him one at a time," Bud admitted, "but we don't figure on doing that. We'll tackle him together. We'll shoot him if he pushes us that far." He dragged the toe of his boot across the floor of the porch. "I know that sounds purty bad, but pa has worked our tails off and he's treated us like little kids. We've finally had enough. If he gets too proddy about the girl, we'll do whatever we have to do, but he ain't bossing us no more, and he sure as hell will never beat any of us again."

Blake shrugged. "Well, I hope you know what you're doing," he said. "If you need any help with him, all you need to do is holler. You boys have got a lot of friends around here. Adam used to have, but not after your ma left. He's run roughshod over too many people."

"What'll we do about the girl?" Bud demanded. "She's

35

awful dirty, so I figure she's been riding a long time and hasn't been cleaned up lately. She probably hasn't had no chance to. I told Luke to heat some water, but if she don't come around, I don't reckon we'd undress her and bathe her."

"It wouldn't hurt you to do it," the doctor said. "If she's that dirty, she's got to have a bath. You won't see nothing that other men haven't seen. I tell you what we'll do. Miranda and me will drive out tomorrow afternoon if I can catch some sleep after the baby comes. If your girl's still unconscious, I'll look her over. All you can do is to keep her in bed. If she's got a concussion and she likely has, she's going to have to be careful for a while."

Bud nodded glumly. "All right, Doc. I want to talk to Miranda."

"Hell, boy, we were just eating supper when you started jerking that bell pull," Blake said in a cranky voice. "Can you let Miranda finish eating?"

"No," Bud said stubbornly. "I've got to see her."

"I'll send her out," Blake said, and disappeared inside the house.

His wife came down the hall a moment later. The doctor's first wife had died a year before and he had married a young woman named Miranda Sturtz about three months later. This had given the Hillcrest gossips a good deal of fuel for their fires. Bud had gone to school with Miranda, so he had known her since she'd been a child. They were almost the same age. He had liked her and as far as he was concerned, her marriage to Doc Blake was their business.

Miranda asked, "What do you want to see me about?"

"We've got a girl at our house who's unconscious," Bud said. "I'm going over to the store and buy everything she needs, but I don't know what all that would be, so I wanted you to make out a list. She's wearing a riding skirt and a shirt, but they're dirty and torn too much to keep on washing 'em."

"I don't know how big she is or whether she's a blond or brunette," Miranda said. "How can I make out a list? I don't even know how old she is."

"I can tell you them things," Bud said. "She's about

36

your age. She's bigger'n you. I'm guessing she'll weigh around one hundred twenty pounds and she's maybe five feet six inches tall. Her hair's brown. Dark brown. Her eyes weren't open, so I don't know what color they are."

Miranda sighed. "All right. Come in and sit down. I'll do the best I can."

"I'll wait out here," Bud said.

She was back in five minutes and handed him a sheet of paper. "That'll have to do for her till you can bring her to town." Miranda hesitated, then said. "If she needs any help from me, just fetch her here. Sometimes a woman needs to talk to another woman and she sure won't find another one on the Big J. Or if you need to know anything you don't know that I can tell, don't be afraid to ask."

"I'll remember," Bud said. "Thanks, Miranda."

He wheeled away and strode back to his horse, thinking there was plenty he didn't know about women, but he was afraid to ask Miranda. He was disappointed that the doctor couldn't see the girl now, but if she wasn't better tomorrow, he'd load her into the wagon and bring her to town. He'd pick her up and carry her into the doctor's house and they could take care of her.

He had trouble with Abe Runkel as soon as he went into the store and handed him the list Miranda had prepared. "You know I can't sell you all this stuff and put it on Adam's bill," Runkel said. "He always takes a close look at everything you boys buy when he's out of town. Last year you bought several items when Adam was gone and he raised hell with me when he got back. He said some of them were expensive luxuries."

"We're all three luxuries he can't afford," Bud said grimly. He put his hands palm down on the counter and leaned forward. "Abe, we've got an injured girl on our hands and we're doing the best we can looking after her. Doc can't come out till tomorrow. I don't know how bad off she is, but whether she's bad off or not, she's got to have these things."

"But Adam will . . ."

"I don't care what he does," Bud said. "We've got to have whatever's on that list. None of us boys have a

37

nickel. Neither has the girl as far as I know. That means you'll charge it to pa. He'll pay."

Runkel shoved the paper across the counter toward Bud. "I'm sorry, son, but I can't . . ."

Bud drew his gun. "Abe, you can put this down as a robbery if you want to and go call the sheriff, but if you don't give me every item that's on that list, I'll fix this store so you won't know it." He cocked his gun. "Now start in."

Abe Runkel looked at Bud's face, then at the gun, and finally at Bud's face again. "All right, but the sheriff is going to hear about it and don't you forget it."

Ten minutes later Bud tied a sack containing his purchases behind the saddle and, mounting, started home. Everything that had happened since he'd come to town simply added to his hatred for his father. He hoped Adam Jones got home soon so they could get the showdown over with and he and Dolan and Luke could ride out and never see the Big J again.

But what would happen to the girl if they did?

Chapter VII

DOLAN JONES leaned his shotgun against the wall beside the bedroom door, pulled up a rocking chair, and sat down. Luke went to bed upstairs, telling Dolan he was a fool for losing a night's sleep. The girl would be all right. Sure, she was scared. She thought she had committed some kind of crime and she was trying to run away, but that didn't mean anybody was going to come in tonight and murder her.

Luke ended up by saying, "You've been readng too many of them Sherlock Holmes' stories till you've got your head all filled up with detectives and murders and stuff like that."

"Maybe I have," Dolan said, "but I've been hoping a woman would show up here and she did. Now I'm not going to take any chances with her."

Luke threw up his hands. "Oh, hell. Go ahead and waste the night if you want to."

"Anyway, I want to be up when Bud gets back with the doc," Dolan said.

By that time Luke was halfway up the stairs. He kept on going and in less than five minutes Dolan heard him snoring. Dolan envied Luke his ability to shed all the problems of life and go to sleep at the drop of a hat. Dolan had never been able to do that. He lay awake for hours almost every night listening to his brothers snore. Luke was the loudest, the most discordant, the most annoying. While they were sleeping, Dolan was lying there thinking about his father, his relationship with his father, and his dreams that would probably never be anything more than dreams.

Of course it wasn't really the snoring that kept Dolan awake. The dreams were mostly to blame. If it wasn't the dreams, it was his problems here and now. Luke and Bud seldom thought about anything except the ranch work or how much they hated their father or what they would do when they left the Big J.

Dolan flattered himself by thinking his mind dwelt on deeper things. For instance, he often asked himself why he was here and what lay ahead after he died. He asked his father once and Adam snorted as if he considered it a damn fool question and said the worms ate you.

Dolan guessed they did, but there was more to him than his long skinny body. The truth was he was afraid to die. That was one reason he had gone to church in Hillcrest when he was younger, but he had discovered that going to church made him more afraid than ever. By the time the preacher got done describing the hell that God had prepared for man, Dolan's stomach was hurting and he quit going to church.

Sometimes he had written poems about life and love and death, but he had never shown them to anyone. He wrote them at night while his brothers were busy snoring. He kept a stubby pencil and a tablet under his pillow and when a poem came to him he would write it down. Of course he couldn't see what he was doing in the dark, and it was hard to make out what he had written when daylight came and he tried to recopy the poem, but he was usually able to get most of it down.

He suddenly came awake with a jerk, then mentally cursed himself for going to sleep in the rocking chair. He had kept the fire up in the range and had put a pot of coffee on, so he got up and filled a cup with coffee and returned to the rocker, all the time listening for any unfamiliar sound from the yard. Now he heard a horse coming in from the south, but he did not hear the jingle of trace chains and the usual squeal of Doc's rig.

Dolan picked up his shotgun and, slipping outside, put his back to the wall. In the starlight he saw the vague shape of a horse and rider going toward the corral. He didn't move, but held his shotgun on the ready. Presently he heard footsteps coming toward the house and he called, "Who is it?"

"Bud." A moment later his brother appeared out of the darkness and stood in the pool of lamplight that fell through the doorway. When Dolan stepped away from the wall and into the light, Bud demanded, "What in the hell are you doing with that shotgun?"

Dolan swallowed, thinking that he had been unduly cautious. He often dreamed up things to be afraid of and his father needled him about his fears. Usually Luke and Bud were more tolerant, but he had a hunch Bud wasn't going to be tolerant now. Maybe if he ignored the question, Bud would forget it.

"Where's the doc?" Dolan asked as he moved back into the house and leaned the shotgun against the wall.

Bud followed. He said, "Doc couldn't come. He's having a baby. He said he'd be out tomorrow if he gets any sleep tonight." Bud laid a package he was carrying on the stand. "I've got some clothes and stuff for her. I don't know what all is in the package. I asked Miranda to make a list and had Abe Runkel fill it, which he done after some persuasion. How is she?"

"She came around," Dolan said, "but she can't remember anything. She doesn't know her name or why she was up here on the mesa or anything."

"The hell!" Bud stared at Dolan and shook his head. "In the morning I'll load her into the buggy and take her to town. The doc had better look her over."

"No," Dolan said sharply. "Leave her here. She feels pretty good except for a headache. She talks fine. She took a bath and Luke gave her one of your shirts and a pair of your pants. Leave her here till she gets on her feet and wants to leave."

Bud scratched the back of his neck, looking at Dolan thoughtfully. "Maybe I'd better. Doc said that she ought to be kept quiet if she's got a concussion and she probably has." He motioned to the shotgun. "Now are you going to tell me what you were doing sitting up and keeping guard with that scattergun."

Bud hadn't forgotten after all. Dolan said, "She's got a feeling she's done something terrible, but she can't remember what it was. She figures maybe she's running away,

41

only she didn't know who or what she was running from. I had a notion that if somebody was really after her, I'd better stand guard till you or Luke got up in the morning."

Bud grinned. "So you're protecting her from whoever is after her. All right, you go ahead. I'm heading for bed. We'll decide in the morning what we'll do with her."

"We're going to leave her here," Dolan said in a sharp tone of authority. "It's a good thing to have a woman on this spread and we are not giving her up. Not for pa or anyone."

Bud had turned toward the stairs, but Dolan's tone of voice brought him around. "Well, now," he said, "has the rabbit grown a mouthful of teeth?"

"I'm no hero and if somebody did come after her, I'd holler for you and Luke to come running," Dolan said, "but I've got a feeling about her. She needs us, and after living here the way we have and being raised by Adam Jones, we sure need her."

"Dolan, sometimes you talk like you know a hell of a lot more than you were ever taught," Bud said. "All right, we'll keep her if she wants to stay. You're right about our needing her, but whether she needs us and the grief that pa's gonna give her is another question."

Bud climbed the stairs. Dolan sat down in the rocker again and leaned his head against the back of the chair. He did know more than he had been taught. He had no idea where the knowledge came from, but he knew a great deal more than he ever talked about.

For one thing, Dolan realized that violence and brute strength the way his father used them did not solve any problems. He knew by the same token that any man needed a woman to be a well-rounded man, or just a good human being. His father's hatred of women had warped him, making him into some kind of two-legged animal who had at times beaten Luke and Bud until he was tired.

Dolan had often thought that a woman might soften or at least mellow his father, and now this young woman who had come out of nowhere was the answer to his prayer. They had to keep her, had to face his father with

42

her in the hope that all of their lives might be straightened out.

Dolan had never quite understood how or why he had escaped the beatings his brothers had received. He did not understand, either, how he could possibly be as inept as he was with the ranch jobs that he was told to do unless it was the fact that he was left-handed and the world was certainly a right-handed one.

In any case, he was very much aware that he was not like Bud and Luke, that for some reason they had protected him from his father since he was a small boy. He had never proved his courage or his manhood. Now he had his chance. In the end he might not have the guts to do what needed to be done, but he was going to try, and he knew the trying would be a step in the right direction.

He was still in the rocking chair at dawn when Luke came downstairs. Luke asked, "Did the doc come?"

"No," Dolan answered, and told him why.

"You go on upstairs and get some sleep," Luke said. "If anybody comes around looking for trouble, I'll oblige them."

Dolan went upstairs and pulled off his boots. Keeping his clothes on, he lay down but he couldn't sleep. He didn't know how he knew, but he was as certain that trouble was on the way as he was of taxes and death.

Chapter VIII

JIM TURNBULL went to bed, but he did not sleep for more than a few minutes at a time. He would drop off, then wake up and feel as if he had slept for hours, but when he struck a match to look at his watch, he would discover he had not slept for more than five or ten minutes.

He didn't feel any guilt about shooting the Kid. The boy deserved to die because of his carelessness with Judy. It was Judy who was on Turnbull's mind. She didn't know the details of the scheme for robbing the store, but she knew they planned to rob the store and that was enough. If the store was filled with armed men and Turnbull led his men into the trap, they'd get wiped out.

For the first time since he'd started riding the owlhoot, Turnbull found himself in a position where he didn't know what to do. Finally, near dawn he rose, and rolled and lighted a cigarette. He pulled the rawhide-bottom chair to the window. He sat down and stared into the dark street below him, wondering why Judy had done what she had.

He was confident he could charm any woman he set his mind to, and he had charmed Judy into running away from home with him. Once they were on the road, he had felt there was no more necessity to keep on charming her.

She was dependent on him and was helpless. For her to ride off into an empty and unknown country was stupid. Anything could happen to her. She might fall into the hands of some men who would be a hell of a lot meaner to her than he had been.

Turnbull had always gone on the premise that first you charm a woman, then you keep her in line by scaring the living hell out of her. He had done exactly that with Judy. In a way, this comforted him because she was probably too scared of him to tell anyone of the plan to rob the store and the chances were good she'd continue to keep her mouth shut for the same reason.

On second thought, Turnbull knew he could not depend on that, so he had to find her before she told anyone. There weren't many ranches up the creek, and certainly she must have found a ranch where she could stay by now. Even if he found the right ranch, he wasn't sure how he could get her away from it without using force.

When it was daylight, he shaved and went downstairs to the dining room for breakfast. The same blonde waitress came to his table who had waited on him the previous morning. He said, "Flapjacks and bacon and a cup of that good coffee of yours."

"Yes, sir," she said, and smiled and wiggled.

He leaned back in his chair and winked at her. Just the presence of a good-looking woman was enough to make the morning brighter than it had been. She wrote his order down, taking more time than she needed and glancing at him over the edge of her pad.

"What's your name?" he asked.

"Susie Eckel," she said. "Folks call me light-headed Susie, but I don't know if they call me that because I'm a blonde or because I act so light-headed."

"I love light-headed girls," he said. "If there's a dance in town Saturday night, I'd like to take you."

"Oh, there is," she said eagerly, "in the Oddfellows Hall over the store. It's a big affair. They call it the prefair dance and all the money goes into prizes for the races."

"Then it's a date?"

"It's a date," she said. "I've got to work until nine that evening, but the dance doesn't start until nine."

"Good," he said, "I'll meet you here."

She nodded. "Wait in the lobby for me."

"I'm Jim Turnbull," he said.

45

She nodded again and smiled. "I've heard about you. You're looking for a horse ranch. Right?"

"Right," he said. "I guess you don't remain a stranger in this town."

"Not usually," she said. "It's different just a few days before the fair. There's stangers all over town then and one of them is about like another. Mostly they're men who come here to race their horses or they're riding in some of the races or they might be just looking for something to gamble on."

She left to take his order to the cook. He leaned back in his chair and rolled and lighted a cigarette, thinking how easy it was to hoodwink a girl like that. Like Judy, too. In a little burg they were likely to be bored and discontented, and all a man had to do was to encourage them and they were all over him.

He laughed silently, telling himself he wasn't exactly humble in his attitude toward women. All he'd had to do since he'd been a teen-age boy was to snap his fingers and the girls came running. Well, maybe not always. He had to admit that, but he had a talent for knowing which ones would come and which ones wouldn't. Light-headed Susie was one who would.

As soon as he finished eating, he got his horse from the livery stable and left town, taking Banner Creek road. He had planned to visit every ranch that was on the creek feeling sure that Judy would be on one of them. If he didn't see her, he could probably spot her bay mare in the corral and know she was there. After that he would decide what to do.

When he was halfway to the camp where he had left the Kid's body, the thought came to him that it would be smart to "discover" it and go back to town and report to the sheriff. No one except Judy knew he had any connection with the boy. If he found the body and reported it to the sheriff, the people in Hillcrest would not have any reason to associate him with the murder. Judy wouldn't have an opportunity to tell anyone, and it was unlikely that she would be believed if she did.

He found the body just as he had left it. He dismounted and walked around as if looking for clues, then he remembered the groceries he had bought from Abe Runkel and

46

realized he had been foolish just to toss them into the willows.

The sheriff might find them and take them to Runkel, who might remember who had bought them. He hunted until he found the gunny sack. He untied it and dropped a rock inside and tied it again, then tossed it into a deep hole. No one would find it there.

He rode back to town and went directly to the old frame courthouse that was centered in an entire block north of the business section. Several ragged cottonwoods shaded the street and yard in front. The building needed paint, and the lawn was not a lawn at all, but an expanse of dog fennel and dandelions and other weeds.

Turnbull tied his horse at the rack under the cotton-woods and strode along the spur-scarred walk to the front door of the courthouse, thinking that the people of this county were like the people of many other counties in the cattle country. The neglected courthouse was a symbol of law and indicated the attitude of the county's citizens toward law.

At first glance, the sheriff seemed to represent that same attitude. He was middle-aged, perhaps fifty, a large man running to fat. His belt was buckled just under the bulging curve of his belly. His name was Ed Drumm, he said as he shook hands with Turnbull. He added that he had heard Turnbull was looking for a horse ranch and he'd be glad to help in any way he could.

Durmm spoke slowly and in a low tone as if he were just too lazy to raise his voice, but his handshake was firm, and Turnbull, who had been fooled before by lazy-appearing law men, decided that there was more behind those gray eyes than he had first thought.

"That's right," Turnbull said. "I'm riding around the country looking it over. This morning I was up Banner Creek about five miles and discovered a body. It was a boy. He'd been murdered. He looked like he was seven-teen or eighteen. I walked around trying to see if the killer had left any sign, but I didn't find a thing. I reckon the rain would have washed out the tracks if he'd left any."

"I reckon it would." Drumm wagged his head, his lazy gray eyes fixed on Turnbull. "A boy, you say? Now who would want to murder a boy?"

47

"I sure can't answer that question for you," Turnbull said. "He'd been shot several times. Any of the bullet holes looked like they'd have killed him."

"Is that so?" Drumm said without the slightest show of interest. Apparently he wasn't surprised at anything Turnbull had said. "Well, sir, a thing like that is done because a man gets plumb carried away by anger or jealousy or some such feeling, but usually it's a woman who gets murdered and her body filled with lead. Thank you kindly, Mr. Turnbull. I'll get a team and wagon and go fetch the body in."

Turnbull turned to the door, then swung back. "Sheriff, what ranches are up Banner Creek? I don't remember seeing any between here and where I found the body."

"No, that's all Anchor range," Drumm said. "Well now, let me see. Anchor's on up the creek another mile or so from where you found the body. You go another five miles to where the valley widens out and you'll find the M Bar. It's a small spread, but it could be a purty good one. Might be for sale. Belongs to a widder woman named Lisa Monroe. The only other spread in that part of the county is the Big J.

"It's on the mesa east of the creek. A road climbs the mesa hill and the ranch buildings are another mile or so farther north. It ain't for sale, though. Belongs to a man named Adam Jones. Right now he's in Denver. Just his three boys at home."

"I'll have a look anyhow," Turnbull said. "You can't always tell what a ranch owner will say if he hears a good offer. I can see Jones after he comes back."

He nodded at Drumm and left the office. He thought he had handled that situation very well, but finding Judy and then deciding how to shut her mouth was a tougher problem.

He visited Anchor first and was asked to stay for dinner. It was a big outfit, bigger than he had expected to find. Drumm had been right. The owner was an Easterner who lived in Boston and seldom visited the ranch. The manager a lantern-jawed cowboy named Stan Oliver said there was no use to even write to the owner.

The M Bar was another matter. It ran to new paint on the house and flowers in the yard. There seemed to be only two cowhands on the place and both were old men. Lisa Monroe was a middle-aged woman who wanted to move to Denver and was almost frantic in her efforts to interest Turnbull in her ranch.

He got away as soon as he could and rode back downstream, thinking that Mrs. Monroe would have come close to giving the outfit away if he had really been serious about buying a ranch. He was relatively sure that Judy was not at either place, so she must have put her mare up the steep mesa hill and gone to the Big J.

Turnbull sighed as he turned off the road to the top of the mesa. He was tired and he wanted to go back to town and get a drink and a good meal and go to bed, but as long as he was this close to the Big J, he'd have a look.

If he didn't find her here, he might consider the possibility that she had somehow been injured or killed during the storm. But he would find her on the Big J, he told himself. He had a hunch, and Jim Turnbull was a man who never doubted a hunch when it was this strong.

He didn't know why it hit him like this unless it was the process of elimination, but as his horse labored up the steep slope to the mesa, he didn't doubt her presence here. The only thing he questioned was how to deal with her.

Chapter IX

JUDY WOKE when Luke built a fire in the kitchen range. A moment later she heard the screen door bang shut and his tall heels crack on the porch and she knew he was going outside to feed the stock. There was silence then, except for the crackling of wood in the range.

For a little while she lay there staring at the ceiling, as she tried to recall who she was and how she happened to be there. She could remember nothing before she came to on the couch last night. She remembered everything after that: Luke and Dolan Jones and her bath and Luke offering to undress her. She remembered Luke saying they had a brother named Bud who had gone to town for a doctor, but no doctor had come to examine her, so Bud must not have brought him back.

She was close to remembering who she was. It would come to her. Something would trigger it and it would all come back to her and she would know who she was and what she had done. She was sure of it. Now she could remember nothing past last night except that she was frightened. She knew she had been running from something. But what? And why? The thought came to her that she might get Luke and Dolan into trouble. She'd have to leave, she told herself. Right after breakfast.

Judy sat up, thinking that the least she could do was to cook breakfast, but she remembered her crackling headache last night. She wasn't sure she could stand on her feet, let alone cook breakfast. As far as leaving was concerned, she had better forget it, at least for a few days.

Slowly she put her feet on the floor and stood up. Her head didn't hurt. Well, yes, it did hurt a little, a dull, throbbing pain, but it was nothing compared to the excruciating agony that had threatened to split her skull last night.

She left the bedroom, walking slowly and carefully, and crossed the front room and went on into the kitchen. She was going to be all right. The only thing wrong with her was the simple fact that she was hungry, she told herself, and that was something she was going to remedy at once.

She filled the firebox with pieces of pine, found coffee and ground it, and put the pot on the front of the stove. She sliced bacon and started it frying, then began to mix a bowl of flapjack dough. She heard someone and turned to see a young man standing by the table looking at her.

This would be Bud, she thought. She had not seen him before. He looked younger than Luke or Dolan. He was not as heavy-set as Luke, and not as tall a Dolan, but he was well built. He had freckles and a snub nose and a rock-like jaw that told her he was a fighter.

"You must be Bud," she said.

"That's right," he said. "Who are you?"

Suddenly she felt as if she wanted to cry. Her hair was a mess and she was wearing Bud's shirt and pants that must make her look awful. She realized immediately that she wanted to look nice for the three Jones brothers more than anything else in the whole world.

"I don't know," she said. "All I know is that I woke up here in this house last night. I can't remember anything before that I . . . I guess I look pretty awful, don't I?"

He grinned. "You could stand a little fixing. I brought some things from the store for you. They're in a package on the stand in the other room. Why don't you go see what's in there. I'll start the flapjacks for you. The doc said you'd have to take it easy for a while. You probably ought to lie down."

"No," she said, "I feel fine."

She hesitated, looking at Bud who came to her and took

51

the tablespoon out of her hand. "Go on," he said, jerking his head at the front room.

She obeyed. Picking up the package, she went into the bedroom and broke the string. Again she felt like crying. Bud had no obligation to go to town and buy these things for her. She found underclothes and stockings and a pink-and-white checked dress. Oh yes, a mirror. Then she discovered a hair brush, hair pins, and a bar of Castile soap. She wouldn't have to use that strong laundry soap after all.

Judy sat on the edge of the bed and brushed her hair. She was still doing it when Bud knocked on the door and called, "The grub's on."

"I'm coming," she said.

Quickly she took off Bud's shirt and pants and dressed in the clothes he had brought. She thought about taking his shirt and pants to him, then decided to keep them. If she stayed here any length of time, the dress would get dirty and she'd have to have something else to wear while she washed it.

The dress was far from being a perfect fit, but it would do. At least it was a dress. She left her hair hanging down her back when she walked out of the bedroom. She saw that Dolan had come downstairs, too. All three boys were sitting at the table in the kitchen. They had started to eat, but when they saw her, they stopped chewing and simply stared.

Bud was the first to recover. He said, "It's a little big, but it fits pretty good, don't it?"

"It's fine," she said. "Thank you very much."

"Come and eat," Bud said. "I guess you're hungry."

"I am," she said, and sat down at the place Bud had set for her.

Dolan had not taken his eyes off her from the instant she had come into the kitchen. Now he blurted, "You are very pretty. We're glad you're here."

She looked at him in surprise. It was the first time she had heard his voice and she was vaguely surprised. It was strong and vibrant, and for some reason she had thought it would be high pitched. She said, "Thank you. I'm glad to be here, but I don't think I'd better stay. I'm afraid I'll get all of you into trouble. I know I'm scared, but I can't remember what I did to be scared of."

"We don't scare easy," Luke said. "You won't get us into trouble. If you do, we can handle it."

"You're staying here till pa gets back," Bud said. "We'll be good to you, but pa won't. He's a . . ." She thought he was going to say his father was a bastard or son of a bitch, but he caught himself. "He's an ornery booger. After you see him, you can decide what you want to do. We're leaving and we'll take you with us if you like us well enough to go. Or we'll take you to town and put you on a train and start you for home."

"I don't think I've got a home," she said. "I can't remember if I have."

"You will remember," Bud said. "It'll come back if you give it enough time. Doc was having a baby last night, but he'll be out today with his wife to see you, if he got any sleep."

Judy began to eat. A moment later Bud and Luke pushed their chairs back, Bud saying, "We've got some riding to do. Dolan will stay with you."

"He doesn't need to stay with me," Judy said. "I'll be all right."

Luke shook his head. "No, I think somebody had better be here with you. Dolan sat up all night with the shotgun so you'd be safe. I think it's something he wants to do."

"That's right," Dolan said. "I do. Not that I'm much good as a fighter, but a shotgun can do a lot of damage to a man even when I pull the trigger."

"As soon as you feel like traveling, we'll take you to town and buy you a pair of shoes," Bud said. "There wasn't any way I could tell the storekeeper how big your feet were."

She shrank back in her chair. "I don't want to go to town. I can go barefoot. If I have to go outside, I can wear my boots."

After they left, Dolan yawned and said he was going to lie down on the couch and for her to wake him if anyone came. Judy cleared the table and washed and dried the dishes. After that she cleaned house, not moving very fast because she was still weak and her head had not completely cleared up.

53

Near noon she went outside and sat down on the porch. She looked at the barn and out-buildings. It was plainly a man's ranch, she thought, built strictly for utility. No flowers, no shade trees, and not even the hint of a lawn in front of the house.

She sighed, thinking it could be made into a very pretty place with a little work. The mesa ran on to the south for miles, with mountain peaks rising against the sky on the east and west. The grass was good and the air was clean and pine scented. Not far to the east of the buildings she saw a slight ridge with a heavy growth of aspen, their small, pale green leaves turning restlessly in the slight breeze.

Maybe they would give her work. If they did, she would stay. They needed a housekeeper. But she didn't know what the boys' father was like. They made no secret of the fact that they didn't get along and Bud had said something about all three of them leaving. There was trouble, she told herself, and that was a shame because this could be such a fine place to live.

Bud had said they would take her with them, but if they were traveling, she didn't want to go. She didn't know why. She didn't want to. She guessed it was because she was tired and it seemed so nice just to sit here and feel the heat of the sun on her body and look at the sky and the grass and the mountains.

Suddenly she stiffened. A man had appeared on the mesa a mile or so to the south. At first he was very small and she wasn't even sure what she saw was a man. When he came closer, she saw she had been right. He was a man and he was coming here.

She went inside and shook Dolan awake. She didn't know why, but she was faintly uneasy and wondered if the man, whoever he was, was coming here because of her. Dolan yawned and rubbed his eyes until she said, "A man's coming."

He jumped up and ran to the front door. He picked up his rifle and stood staring at the approaching rider for several minutes, then he said in surprise, "Why, it's Ed Drumm, the sheriff. I wonder what brings him out here. He's not a man to ride this far unless he's got something on his mind."

Dolan stepped through the door and crossed the yard. Watching, Judy had trouble breathing. She put a hand to her throat, her heart pounding. She knew what he wanted. He had come to get her, but she still could not remember what she had done.

Chapter X

LUKE and Bud took salt to the north end of the mesa and decided the grass would hold up until their father got back from Denver. It would be up to him to decide whether he would move the cattle or leave them where they were. The men did not talk much as they rode, but they touched up their horses on the way back, hoping to get to the house by noon.

When they were within fifty yards of the house, Luke asked, "Is she gonna remember who she is? Or is she faking it?" He shook his head glumly. "How is it going to end?"

"I don't think she's faking it," Bud answered. "She'll remember, all right, but I dunno when it'll be. I hope Doc gets out to see her. Maybe he'll know what to do."

"Hell," Luke grumbled, "we don't even know what to call her."

"We'll call her Sis," Bud said, "seeing as we don't know her name."

"Sis?" Luke laughed. "It won't do for Dolan. He's got romantical notions about her now before we even know whether she's married or not."

"It'll be good for him," Bud said. "He might even get around to kissing her before she leaves."

"Naw," Luke said. "He won't come no nearer to kissing her than I will." He patted his horse on the shoulder. "And I'd just as soon kiss old Pete here as kiss that girl."

"You're a bachelor," Bud said. "Kissing can be a lot of fun."

Luke snorted. "I suppose you speak from a lifetime of experience."

"Certainly," Bud said in a lofty tone.

They rode around the corner of the house and saw the sheriff, Ed Drumm, talking to Dolan. They reined to a stop, surprised. Bud put up his hands. "Don't shoot, Sheriff. I'll go peaceable."

"It's me he wants," Luke said. "I've been afraid Ed would get out here ever since I held up that stage down on the Grand."

"Cut out the horse play and shut up," Dolan said. "Get down. Ed wants to talk to us and he wants to see our visitor."

Luke and Bud dismounted. Bud said, "Let's go inside. It's hot out here."

Drumm nodded toward the mountains to the east. "It's gonna blow up another gullywasher," he said. "Wasn't that a good one we got yesterday?"

"Too good," Bud said. "It played hell with our road leading off the mesa."

They went into the house. The girl was not in sight. Dolan looked in the kitchen, but she wasn't there, either. Bud nodded at the bedroom door which was closed. He said, "She's probably in there."

Dolan knocked. When there was no answer, he knocked again, harder this time. The girl asked, "What is it?"

"Come on out," Dolan said.

"No. I don't feel very well. My head aches."

Dolan turned to Drumm. "I guess you'll have to come back, Ed. She was bad hurt when she fell off her horse. She must have hit her head on a rock."

"Get her out here," Drumm said. "I didn't make this ride for nothing."

"She'll come out if I have to drag her," Bud said, and strode to the door. He raised his voice, "The sheriff's here and he wants to talk to you. It's a long ride from town, so he ain't likely to come again. That means we'll take you to see him if you don't talk to him now, so you'd better get out here."

57

She opened the door and shot a frightened glance at Drumm. Bud was sorry he'd used the tone he had, but he thought it was easier for her to talk to Drumm today than to have to go to town to see him. He took her hand as he said, "Ed won't hurt you. Sit down." He pulled up a rocker and she sat down. "Just take it easy. I expect he wants to ask you a few questions."

"That's right," Drumm said, his gaze fixed on her pale face. "I've got no intentions of hurting you, Miss . . ."

"Dunn," she said, and showed her surprise. "That's my name. Judy Dunn. I remembered." She laughed nervously, and added, "It just came to me then. Now I'll know what to call myself if I start talking to me. You'll know what to call me instead of 'Hey you.'"

Her gaze touched Dolan's face, then quickly dropped to the floor. Bud, watching her, felt she gave her feeling for him away in that glance. Dolan must have sensed it, too, because his face had turned fiery red when Bud looked at him.

"It's the first thing she's remembered since she came to," Dolan said to Drumm. "That was last night. Maybe she's going to remember some other things."

"I'm sure she will," Drumm said in his lazy way, not taking his eyes off the girl for a second. "Now it strikes me real funny. Here's a girl who's a stranger in these parts. She rides up onto your mesa from Banner Creek and gets bucked off her horse and knocked out. You boys fetch her home, knowing Adam will raise hell and prop it up with a chunk when he gets back and finds her living here with you."

"What are you trying to say, Ed?" Bud demanded. "If it's what I think it is, I don't like it."

"No, I didn't figure you would," Drumm said. "There's a couple of things I'm thinking. One is that you boys knew her from somewhere else and asked her to come here, though you may not have known when she was coming."

"You're clean off the track," Luke said angrily. "None of us ever set eyes on her before we found her late yesterday afternoon. How could we? You know damned well we've never in our lives been out of this county.

58

What's more, you know pa never give us a nickel to go sashaying around any farther away than Hillcrest."

Drumm ignored Luke's outburst. He went on, "The second thing I'm thinking is that she's faked this forgetting business."

"I didn't," Judy said angrily. "I haven't enjoyed not knowing who I am any more than Dolan and his brothers have."

Drumm had been standing near the door. Now he walked toward Judy, and when he was two steps away, he bellowed, "Maybe you can remember the name of the boy you murdered."

Startled, Dolan said angrily, "You hold on, Ed. You've got no call to perform that way. What makes you think she murdered anybody?"

"A man named Jim Turnbull discovered the kid's body this morning," Drumm said. "He's a stranger who's riding around hunting a horse ranch to buy. He rode up Banner Creek and happened to see the body. Chances are he's the only rider who's gone by there since the murder. I figure this girl wouldn't have ridden off the road and come up here in country she didn't know, unless she'd done something like killing this kid. They're both strangers. We don't have no idea why they were camped down there on the road by the creek, but I'm guessing they had a fight and she filled him full of lead."

"What?" Judy cried.

"You shot him five times," Drumm said. "Nobody shoots and keeps on shooting into a dead man unless they've panicked. That's why you got on your horse and took the first side road you saw."

"I didn't shoot him," Judy said. "I don't own a gun. I hit him with a club on the head."

"Ohhhh," Drumm said softly, "now we're remembering."

"Yes," she said. "I remembered about hitting him when I remembered my name. I wanted to get away and he wouldn't let me, so I hit him when his back was turned. If somebody else shot him, I must not have killed him."

Everyone was silent for a long moment. Judy stared at the floor. Dolan looked as if he were going to be sick. Drumm was plainly puzzled. Luke was uneasy. Bud was the only one who wasn't upset. He knew the girl was telling the truth because he had seen the boy trying to start a fire after the storm. He almost blurted that out, then decided to wait until he heard what she would say.

But she wasn't going to say any more, so Drumm asked, "You were in love with him and you'd been traveling together, but he wouldn't let you go."

"No, no," she cried, "I hated him."

"Who is he?" Drumm asked. "What's his name?"

"I don't know." She lowered her head and started to cry. "I tell you I don't know. I never heard him called anything but Kid."

"But you were traveling with him?"

"Yes."

"Why? What were you doing here?"

"We came to see the fair."

"You've got the gall to sit there and tell me you were traveling with this boy and didn't even know his name?"

Drumm scratched his head as if not knowing what to do. Bud decided this was the time to tell Drumm what he knew, though he doubted that the sheriff would believe him. He said, "Ed, I can testify that she didn't kill this boy. I went to town late yesterday afternoon to get the doc for her and buy her some things. I passed the kid's camp. It was just below where our mesa road hits the main Banner Creek road, ain't it?"

"That's right," Drumm said.

"The boy was trying to build a fire after the storm and he wasn't having any luck," Bud said. "When I left here, she was still unconscious on the couch. She's never left the house since we brought her home."

"By God, this girl has hypnotized you," Drumm said in disgust. "Right now I'm leaving her with you 'cause we don't have no place in town to keep women prisoners. I'll hold you boys responsible for her. See she don't run off."

"She won't," Dolan said.

Drumm strode to the door, then turned and glared at Bud. He said, "I've known all of you boys from the day you was born, and I never had one of you lie to me before."

60

Drumm wheeled and left the house. He mounted and, scowling, looked down at Bud and Luke who had followed him across the yard. "If you get anything more out of her, come to town and tell me, if you can tell the truth from now on."

"You don't have any real evidence against her," Bud said. "How about the fellow who found the body?"

"Turnbull?" Drumm shook his head. "He wouldn't have reported finding the body if he'd killed the kid."

Drumm rode away Bud stared at his back for a time, then he asked, "What do you think, Luke?"

"I think we've got trouble on our hands," Luke said grimly.

Bud nodded. "That's exactly what I think."

Chapter XI

JUDY cooked dinner, and as soon as they finished eating, she said, "You skedaddale now, all of you. I'm going to clean house and you'll just be underfoot if you're in here. I've never seen such a dirty place in all my life."

They got up from the table, embarrassed. Dolan said, "I guess we ain't much good as housekeepers. It's my fault the house is in such a mess. I'm supposed to take care of . . ."

"I'm not blaming any of you," Judy broke in. "You're men and men don't know how to keep a house clean. This is woman's work and I'm glad to get at it." She hesitated, looking at Luke, then Dolan, and finally at Bud. "The truth is I want to show you what a woman can do around here and then maybe you'll let me stay and keep house for you. I don't have anywhere else to go."

"You still don't remember where you came from or why you're here or who the kid was you hit over the head?" Bud asked.

She couldn't meet his gaze. She shook her head and whispered, "No, I can't remember anything else."

"We can't let you stay here when Pa gets back from Denver," Luke said. "It ain't that we don't want you, but Pa, well, he just won't have a woman on the place and that's a fact."

"Pa's a bad one," Dolan added. "He's so bad that we're fixing to leave home right after he gets back. Bud's gonna be twenty-one in a little while and there won't be nothing he can do to make us stay."

They turned to the back door. Bud paused there and said, "Judy, I ain't sure you ought to be working like this after getting the wallop you did. Doc will be out purty soon. Or if he don't make it, we'll take you to town to see him. We'll know more what you ought to be doing after he has a look at you."

"I'm all right," she said. "I've just got a little headache now. If I get too tired, I'll stop and rest. I promise I will."

"All right," Bud said reluctantly and turned toward the door again.

"Oh, Mr. Jones . . ." Judy began.

Bud stopped the second time and looked at her. He said, "Bud. Pa is Mr. Jones and he ain't here."

She bit her lip, her face turning red. She wanted to do everything right and she seemed to be doing everything anything but right. "Bud, there isn't much in the pantry to eat. Just beans and potatoes and ham and bacon and flour. Oh, and a little sugar. Some coffee, too."

Bud seemed puzzled. "Well, that's the kind of stuff we've eaten all our lives," he said.

"I like to cook," she said, "but I can't make much variety if that's all you've got. This is a cattle ranch. You ought to have beefsteak to eat."

Bud laughed softly. "We have got red meat to eat if one us fetches in some venison. Or an elk. Or even a rabbit. But beefsteak? No, Pa says we can't afford it. We sell our cattle. Besides, some of the meat might spoil in hot weather, but bacon and ham will keep."

"You can afford to butcher, can't you?" she asked.

"Oh, Pa's a rich man, but he says he wouldn't be if we ate up our cattle, and we don't have any neighbors who run stock on our range, so we can't steal anybody else's beef."

"Your Pa's not here," she said sharply, looking directly at him now. "Why don't you and your brothers go out and butcher a steer? Bring the liver in for supper."

"Well, now," Bud said thoughtfully, "maybe we will. There's a yearling we seen this morning that's been limping around. We'll go find him."

After he left, she pumped several buckets of water and filled the reservoir and the tea kettle, then brought the

63

boiler in from the back porch and set it on the front of the stove and filled it with water. She built up the fire and, finding the wood box empty, she went out through the back door to the woodpile just as the three brothers rode away.

She chopped an armload of wood and returned to the house. She washed the dishes and stripped the beds, then washed and hung the blankets on the line to dry. There was enough work to keep her busy until Christmas, she told herself, but she didn't know what she could do to change the brothers' minds about letting her stay.

Somehow she couldn't believe their father was as bad as they claimed he was. Judging from what they had said, their father was very stingy, so his attitude toward women was probably due to his reluctance to pay a housekeeper.

If she could show him how different the house and meals and their clothes would be with her working here, and if she could convince him she would work for board and room, maybe she could persuade him to let her stay.

She started scrubbing the kitchen floor, and then, in spite of herself, her thoughts turned to Jim Turnbull. She was remembering all that had happened. It came slowly at first; her perfectionist mother who had never been satisfied with the work she'd done, her father who drank too much and often beat both her and her mother, and finally Jim Turnbull who rode into the community and seemed to be such an honest, responsible man, but who had turned out to be a bank robber.

She told herself bitterly she had done exactly as thousands of girls had done, but she had been dead wrong. No matter how bad her home had been, it had never been as bad as the life she had lived since she'd run away with Turnbull. Now she was under suspicion of a murder that Turnbull had probably committed, but she couldn't bring herself to tell the sheriff or the Jones brothers how it had been with her and Turnbull.

If she couldn't stay here, where would she go? What would she do? She could not go home. She would not and could not go back to Jim Turnbull.

Her headache had gotten much better, but now as the

worry about her future took hold of her, it grew until there was no room in her mind for anything else. The headache returned, and for a while she thought her head would split.

Late in the afternoon the brothers rode back into the yard, Luke carrying the carcass of a yearling they had butchered. A moment later Dolan came into the kitchen with the liver. He laid it in a pan and looked at Judy in his shy way.

"We don't usually eat livers," he said, "but I reckon we can try it once."

She smiled at him. "It will be good. I promise."

"You'd better quit work and go into the other room," Dolan said. "The doc and his wife are coming. I seen their buggy just before I got to the house. It'll be another ten minutes before they get here."

"Thank you," she said. "Will you chop some wood for me, please? I was going to, but I guess I'd better pin my hair up."

"Sure I will," he said. "That's my job. I just forgot it when we left at noon."

She moved quickly to the mirror on the wall beside the sink and took her hair down. She brushed it quickly and pinned it up again. She had barely finished when Luke and Bud came into the house with Doc Blake and his wife.

Bud introduced them, and Miranda Blake said, "Why, Miss Dunn, your dress fits you quite well, considering."

"Yes," Judy said, smiling faintly. "Considering."

"Don't worry your pretty head about it," Blake said. "These boys are so hungry to have a woman around the place that they won't notice whether your dress fits or not."

Miranda turned to Bud. "You'll have to drive her to town tomorrow. She needs a change of clothes, and she can find some dresses that fit her better than this one if she has a chance to try them on."

"She don't have no money," Bud said. "We don't, neither. I charged these and Pa is gonna raise hell and shove a chunk under it when he finds out."

"If you'd just let me stay here and work," Judy said, "I'd take the clothes for my wages."

65

Luke threw up his hands. "We keep telling her what Pa's like, but she don't believe us. Maybe she never seen a bullhead like him."

"If she hasn't seen one like him," Miranda Blake said, "she wouldn't believe he's real."

The doctor nodded his agreement. "She's right. You never met a man like him because the good Lord wouldn't be ornery enough to let two men like him be born. Well now, girl, Bud tells me you got throwed off your horse."

"I guess so," Judy said. "I don't rightly know what happened. I ride pretty well, but I was tired. My mare shied at something and I guess she threw me. I think I remember a rabbit jumping out of the brush right in front of me. All I remember for sure is lying on the couch when I came to last night."

Blake had set his black bag on the oak stand in the center of the room. "You come on over to the couch and lie down. I'll have a look at you. How do you feel?"

"I've worked all afternoon," she said, "so I can't be very bad off."

He glanced around the room and nodded. "Chances are this is the first time in fifteen years that the floor's been scrubbed. At least you didn't faint and fall into your mop water, but you didn't answer my question."

"I've still got a headache," she committed.

"That's natural," he said. "Chances are you'll have one for a while."

He felt her pulse and listened to her heart, then carefully ran his fingertips over the bump on her head. "Tender, isn't it?" he asked.

"Real tender," she agreed.

He stepped back and scratched the tip of his nose. "It's a little hard to tell how much of a wallop you got, but since you've worked like a horse all afternoon, I don't think you are very bad off. Nothing to do except let nature heal you. Just be careful that you don't try working all day and overdo. Half a day is about what you'd better work."

She sighed. "There's so much to do in this house, and I want Mr. Jones to see how improved it is when he gets home."

"If you shined this house up so it put his eyes out when he came in, he wouldn't know you had done a thing," Blake said bluntly. "Now you just forget about working for Adam Jones."

Miranda had sat down in a rocking chair. Now she leaned forward and said, "Judy ... you don't mind me calling you Judy?"

"No, of course not."

"What I started to say was that after Adam gets back, if you and the boys are still alive, have one of them drive you into town. I'll give you a job. You won't find our house as dirty as this one, but it's kind of dirty. The doctor married me a while back thinking I was a spic and span housekeeper, but I had him fooled."

"She did for a fact," Blake grunted. "Bud, when she feels like traveling, fetch her to town and buy her all the clothes she needs. Charge it to me. No use of you getting into any more trouble with Adam than you already are."

"Thank you," Judy said faintly.

There were more good people in the world than she had ever guessed. She wondered why she had to ride all these miles to find them.

Chapter XII

Doc Blake moved to the fireplace and stood in front of it while he filled and lighted his pipe. He tossed the charred match into the fireplace and for a time talked to Luke about the weather and the range and the price of beef. Dolan had brought in several armloads of wood and now stood in the kitchen doorway listening.

Bud, too, listened, but with only half an ear. He kept looking at Judy, his mind filled with questions about her. Dolan had fallen in love with her after knowing her only a few short hours. That was like Dolan, Bud thought. He didn't need a woman to sleep with as much as Luke and Bud did, but he did need a woman to talk to, to do things for him, to somehow make his world a little more gentle than he had known on the Big J. Bud wasn't sure Judy Dunn was the woman for that. He wasn't even sure she was honest.

The thought stirred Bud's mind that maybe they would all be better off if they sent her back to town today with Doc and Miranda, but he knew Dolan would raise hell. Luke wasn't very sensitive about these things and he wouldn't understand, but Bud told himself fiercely that if the girl hurt Dolan in any way, he'd break her neck.

Doc knocked his pipe out into the palm of his hand and threw the ash into the fireplace. "Well, Miranda, we'd best be heading for home. You've still got some housecleaning to do."

"See how he cracks the whip?" Miranda asked. "All right, my lord. Let's get back to the salt mines."

The doctor laughed, but Bud had a feeling that he had been half serious. Blake went outside and crossed to the buggy, the others streaming behind him. Bud said, "Much obliged for coming out this afternoon."

Blake nodded as he started to untie his horse. "Glad to," he said. "I needed to get out of town after being up all night with . . ."

A rifle cracked from the quaking aspens on the slope above them. Bud heard the report and looked up in time to see the puff of smoke from the edge of the trees and then he was aware that Judy had cried out. He whirled back toward her as she reached for the buggy seat, but she was too far away. She started to fall. Bud was closer to her than anyone else and he jumped forward, his arms outstretched. He caught her just before she hit the ground.

"Git for the house," Luke yelled.

The rifle cracked again, the slug kicking up a geyser of dirt in front of Bud as they ran back to the house. He was the first through the door. Crossing the room, he laid her on the couch.

"I'm all right," she said. "The first shot nicked my leg. That's all."

The rest were in the room now, Blake pushing her skirt up on her thighs to look at the wound. Bud saw the blood that made a spreading red stain on her calf. He said, "Come on, Luke. Grab your Winchester and let's get that bastard."

"Fetch me some hot water, Miranda," Blake ordered. "It's not a bad wound, but I'd better wash off the blood and bandage it."

Bud and Luke grabbed their rifles off the antler rack near the front door. Again the rifle cracked, the bullet splintering the door casing. "Through the back," Bud said. "He'll smoke us down if we go out this way, but we might get to the corral the other way."

Judy sat up, crying, "Don't go. He'll kill you."

They didn't stop to argue with her, but raced through the kitchen and across the back porch. Only then did Bud realize he hadn't even thought of telling Dolan to come.

When they were in the open, Bud bent low and sprinted toward the corral, expecting the dry gulcher to open up again, but there was no other shot. They saddled up, jammed their rifles into the boots, and mounted. They rode straight toward the aspens, Bud perfectly aware that they might be shot out of their saddles any second, but he had a hunch that the rifleman had fled, or he would have started shooting the moment they came into view from the back of the house.

A few minutes later he saw he was right. They reached the trees and swung down. Pulling their Winchesters from the scabbards, they plunged into the aspens. Within a matter of seconds, Bud called, "Luke! This is where he was lying."

Bud pointed to the grass that plainly showed someone had been lying there for some time. Three spent 30-30 shells were on the ground along with half a dozen cigarette stubs. Luke nodded and moved on into the trees. A moment later he called to Bud that he'd found the place where the man had left his horse. Bud joined him, noting the piles of horse manure and the tromped-down grass.

"He was here quite a while," Bud said, "but when he saw us take after him, he didn't want no more of it. What do you make of this business?"

Luke stared at him, troubled. "I dunno if I want to say what I make of it."

"You mean on account of Judy?" Bud asked.

Luke nodded. "Hell, yes. I don't want to be unfair to her. It's mighty damned good to have her around and she's done a lot for Dolan. She can make a man out of him if she'll do it."

"Go on," Bud pressed. "Say what you're thinking because I've got a hunch I'm thinking the same thing."

Still Luke hesitated. Finally he said, "Well, the son-of-a-bitch might have shot the wrong one. Maybe he aimed to get one of us or the doc, and it just happened by accident that Judy caught the slug."

"Come off it," Bud snapped. "Nobody would shoot Doc or Miranda, and I don't know of anybody who'd shoot one of us or have any reason to. Pa, maybe, if he was here, but he ain't. The question is why would anybody want to shoot a girl like Judy?"

"I dunno." Luke wheeled away and strode toward his horse, calling back, "I don't want to think about it. I guess I want Judy to stay as bad as Dolan does."

70

"I want her to stay, too," Bud said, catching up with Luke, "but we've got to think on it."

"Why?"

"On account of Dolan," Bud said. "Us, too, maybe. This killer, whoever he is, may try again. Next time he might start smoking us down for taking care of Judy."

Luke reached his horse, then stood there, the reins in his hands. "All right," he said heavily, "I ain't much worried about him smoking us down, but I dunno 'bout Dolan. Sometimes he makes me think of a little boy we've got to look after."

"He's no little boy, but we've looked after him as long as I can remember," Bud said, "and we're going on looking after him for a while. Now what are you thinking?"

Luke stepped into the saddle, then shook his head. "I dunno. I ain't very smart on some things. You know that. It don't make no sense that a man . . . any man . . . would try to murder a girl. If you know why, you'd better tell me."

"Of course I don't know," Bud said, half angry at Luke's failure to reach the same conclusion he had, "but the only way it makes sense to me is that Judy must know more than she's told us, like how and why that kid was killed. We know she didn't do it, but she maybe knows who did do it, so the killer figures he's got to shut her mouth. He don't know whether she's told him anything or not, but he does know that if she's dead, she can't testify against him."

Bud mounted and they rode back to the corral, Luke remaining silent until they swung down from their mounts, then he said, "Makes sense, all right, but what do we do now? I don't reckon we can send her back to town with Doc and Miranda."

"Not yet," Bud agreed, "though I've got a hunch that's what we will do before Pa gets home. I was thinking that if Doc would spread the word around town that Judy's lost her memory, maybe this killer will let her alone."

Luke nodded. "Good idea."

They stripped the gear from their horses and turned them into the corral, and going back into the house, returned the Winchesters to the antler rack. Judy was lying on the couch, a tight bandage on her bullet wound.

"Well?" Blake demanded. "You find him?"

"He didn't hang around," Bud said. "We found where he'd been lying and where he left his horse. He took off through the quakies and was gone long before we got there."

"You took a damn fool chance," Dolan said, "rushing up there like you done. If he'd stayed where he was, he'd have knocked you kicking before you got halfway to the quakies."

"Maybe so," Bud said, "but I figured after we ran to the corral and he didn't shoot that he'd pulled out. Besides, we couldn't leave him there. It wouldn't have been safe to have stepped out of the house, Hell, we'd be bottled up here till dark."

Judy was looking at him closely. She asked, "You think it's safe to leave now?"

"Yes, but you're staying inside," he said. "Looks like you're the one he wants to kill. He's gone now, but he might be back tomorrow or the next day. That's why you're staying inside. We'll see to it that one of us is around here all the time."

Bud walked to the couch and looked down at her. He didn't think she would tell the truth yet, but he had to ask again. "Judy, are you sure you can't remember any more than you've told us?"

"Damn it, Bud, quit nagging her," Dolan said. "She's got a headache, she's tired, and she's been shot, and you keep . . ."

"It's all right, Dolan," Judy said, closing her eyes. "No, I can't remember anything more than I've told you."

She was lying just as he had been sure she would, Bud told himself, but Dolan was right. He couldn't press her now. He asked, "Got any idea why this fellow wanted to kill you."

"No."

Doc Blake snapped his bag shut. "I guess we can start again and not get shot at this time. Stay off that leg tonight. It's just a superficial wound, but you might start the bleeding if you walk on it tonight."

"She can stay where she is," Dolan said. "I'll get supper."

72

"Good," Blake said. "And the housecleaning can go till morning. Don't work at it then even if you feel like it. Have one of the boys drive you into town to see me if anything goes wrong, but I don't think it will."

"I'll be fine," she said wearily, "but I do want to get this house cleaned up before Mr. Jones gets home. Maybe he's not as bad as you're making out."

Nobody argued with her this time. Bud and Luke followed Blake and Miranda to their buggy. When they reached it, Bud said, "We thought it would be a good idea if you let it out that there's a strange girl staying here who's lost her memory."

Doc Blake thought about it a moment, glanced at Miranda who nodded as if she understood, then he said, "All right. I'll get me a drink or two tonight and let that little piece of information slip."

"Just hold that to a drink or two," Miranda said severely.

Blake winked at Luke as he stepped into the buggy. "Yes, my love," he said.

They drove away. Luke and Bud stood watching them for a time, then Bud said, "Sometimes I think Judy would be a match for Pa. She's just about as bullheaded as he is."

"Maybe we'd better let her stay," Luke said. "Might be quite a tussle."

"You sure you want to see it?" Bud asked.

"No, I ain't sure," Luke said, "but it might be one way of taking Pa down a notch. Likewise, it might give us an excuse to pull our freight."

"It might at that," Bud agreed. "I was all for getting rid of her the day before he gets home, but what you're saying is that we need an excuse to leave or we won't never do it."

Luke nodded. "If Pa even laid a hand on Judy, Dolan would tackle him by himself."

"I believe he would," Bud agreed. "Well, let's think on it."

The more Bud thought about it, the more he was convinced that Luke was right. The old habit of obeying Adam Jones was so strong that it would take something like him beating Judy to force them to break it.

73

Chapter XIII

AFTER SHOOTING Judy, Jim Turnbull fled from the aspen grove and rode back to town. He did not know whether he had killed Judy Dunn or not. He had seen her start to fall; he had seen one of the men catch her and carry her into the house, so he knew he had scored a hit, but he had no idea how bad it was.

A woman would go down with no more than a scratch from a bullet, from fear if nothing else. It was possible he had not hit her at all, that she had simply fainted. All he knew for sure was that it was time to move; there was nothing to be gained by remaining and fighting it out with a couple of cowhands.

As soon as he reached Hillcrest, he left his horse in the livery stable and went to his room. For a time he lay on the bed and stared at the ceiling, turning his problem over in his mind. And he did have a problem. If Judy was alive and if she told all that she knew about him, the sheriff would be after him pronto.

The law man couldn't prove anything; it would be Judy's word against his, but he'd probably he held in jail and the sheriff would go through his reward dodgers, and the chances were he'd find out that Jim Turnbull was a wanted man. Or, if he didn't, he would certainly hold Turnbull in jail until after the fair was over, and by that time it would be too late to rob the store.

His men might try it without him, but the store would be heavily guarded, simply as a precaution, and the result would be failure. Chances were, some of his men would be killed to boot. The safest thing was to ride out of town now while he could. He'd better camp somewhere outside town and intercept one of his men as he rode by. He'd tell the man how it was and he could pass the word to the others that the deal was off.

That was the safest way, all right, but Jim Turnbull had never been a man to take the safest route. He turned the coin over and examined the other side. Even if Ed Drumm knew who he was and tried to arrest him, Turnbull was confident he could outdraw the man and kill him.

He would get away in the confusion that followed the sheriff's death and he wouldn't be any worse off than if he got out of town now and camped somewhere along the river. He'd never had much fear of cowtown law men, particularly when they were middle-aged and running to fat as Ed Drumm was.

On the other hand, suppose Judy didn't talk. If she had received a friendly welcome on this ranch where she'd gone, she might decide to stay and work. More than likely she wouldn't want to admit she had run away from home and had been living with a man the way she had, a man who had turned out to be a bank robber at that.

He laughed a little when he thought about it. She probably wouldn't talk about herself at all because if she once started, she'd wind up telling the whole story. It was funny as hell, he thought. The girl was no better than a run-of-the-mill whore, but she would certainly pretend to be a very moral girl to people who didn't know her.

Judy, of course, would guess he had killed the Kid and had tried to kill her. She might identify him simply to protect herself, thinking that he would make another attempt on her life. She could identify him easily enough by his name. He'd used a dozen names over the years, but she knew him as Turnbull and he had used that name here in Hillcrest, not knowing when he'd registered at the hotel that he would have any need to change his name.

She might be too scared of him to identify him and take the attempt on her life as a warning. Too, there was a possibility he had hit his target exactly where he had wanted to and she was dead. In any case, the only thing to do now was to play it out. There was no substitute for a good bluff. If she was dead, the news would soon be all over town and he'd hear. If the sheriff had learned anything from her, Turnbull would soon know that, too.

Now that he had made his decision, he rose, poured water from the pitcher into the bowl on his bureau and washed. He combed his hair, checked his gun just on the chance Ed Drumm might try to arrest him, and went downstairs to the dining room. It was dark by the time he finished eating and drifted into the bar for a drink.

He bought a cigar and lighted it, enjoying the taste of it before he ordered his drink. After it came, he stood motionless at the bar, puffing slowly on his cigar and not doing anything which would draw attention to him. He began to turn the whisky glass with the tips of the fingers of his left hand, his right at his side close to the butt of his gun.

A dozen or more men were strung along the bar. He listened to the casual talk. Some were cowboys, some were townsmen, and a few were drummers who were stopping overnight in Hillcrest. The talk was mostly about the approaching fair and the bets the men were going to make.

Turnbull was still standing there when Ed Drumm came in and walked to the bar and ordered a drink. He stood only a few feet from Turnbull who picked up his glass and moved toward him. He had no idea why the sheriff had come into the bar, but it was always a good move to get the jump on the man who might be your enemy, and Ed Drumm certainly would be his enemy if Judy had talked.

"Find out anything more about the boy who was killed?" Turnbull asked. "Or who killed him?"

Drumm looked at him sharply. Turnbull wasn't sure whether the sheriff didn't recognize him for a moment or if he suspected that Turnbull had something to do with the killing. "No," Drumm said, "nothing so far." He had his drink, nodded to several of the men, and walked out.

Turnbull took the half-smoked cigar out of his mouth and examined it critically. Something had been wrong with the way Drumm had acted, but he couldn't identify it. Just a feeling, maybe. He decided he was a little more

76

jumpy than he thought he was. No, it was more than a feeling, he decided after he thought about it. Drumm was suspicious of him, but not suspicious enough to make an arrest. Turnbull didn't know what that meant if it was true.

Other men drifted into the bar. One of them was called Doc, so Turnbull guessed he was the local medico. The man found his place at the bar along the mahogany a few feet from Turnbull. The bartender served him immediately and Turnbull noticed that he was treated with great respect by everyone who knew him.

"I was out to the Big J this afternoon," the doctor said after he'd had his drink. "You boys know what Adam Jones thinks of women. I guess everybody in the country knows. He's talked about it enough. Well sir, the damnedest thing has happened. Adam's in Denver right now and the boys have a young woman with them out there. A mighty pretty young filly too. Now what do you suppose Adam will say when he finds out about it?"

His neighbors along the bar who had heard what he said laughed. One of them, a young cowboy, answered, "He'll beat hell out of all three of his boys."

"I dunno that he'll beat Bud up very much," one of the others, a clerk in Runkel's store, said. "That boy's tougher'n a boot heel. I had trouble with him here in town one day, so I know. It's my guess he's mean enough to pull a gun on his pa."

"I don't know if you'd call that mean," Doc said. "Hell, if anybody's mean, it's Adam. I know the boys pretty well. I'm surprised they've stood that old stud horse as long as they have."

"One thing's sure," the cowboy said. "If Adam had been home, the boys would never have got that girl into the house, no matter how purty a filly she is."

"How'd they find the girl?" the other man asked.

"Well sir, you won't believe what happened," Doc answered. "It would take a man with a wild imagination to think up a yarn like this, but I guess it's true. The boys say they were headed home after Adam got on the train to go to Denver and they found this girl lying on the ground beside the road, knocked cold. Apparently she'd been thrown by her horse. Anyhow, they picked her up and

77

took her home. Bud came to town after me, but I was having a baby and I couldn't go right then. Miranda and me went out there this afternoon. Those Jones boys are treating her like she's an angel. Maybe she is as far as I know."

"That's a purty wild yarn for a fact," the cowboy said. "Now I've often dreamed about finding a purty girl out in the brush, but I never did."

The store clerk snickered. "You wouldn't know what to do with a girl if you found one in the brush, would you, Slim?"

"Sure I would," the cowboy. "If she showed me what she had, I'd know what to do with what I had."

"Where'd the girl come from, Doc?" the clerk asked. "Who is she?"

"She can't remember," Doc answered. "She got a hell of a wallop on her head when the horse threw her and she's lost her memory. She's been working like a fool cleaning up their dirty house, but she can't remember nothing."

Turnbull tossed his cigar stub into a nearby spittoon, relief rushing through him. A great many things were explained. Judy couldn't tell anything about him if she'd lost her memory. It might come back. He'd heard of it happening, but that was a chance he would take. For the moment anyway he was safe. Judy couldn't tell something she couldn't remember.

Turnbull started to turn from the bar, thinking he'd go to his room, when the store clerk said, "That fool Adam just don't have no sense. It ain't only the way he thinks about women, but I've heard that he's got all his money buried somewhere around the house. Or maybe it's hidden inside the house. I don't know. Anyhow, you'd think he'd bank it in Grand Junction. Or even in Denver. He goes out there at least once a year and sometimes more'n that."

"I heard that, too," the cowboy said. "Maybe ten, fifteen thousand dollars. He works the tar out of his boys and don't pay 'em nothing. Luke and Bud are good hands, too. He never buys nothing he don't have to, but he ships a fine bunch of beef every year."

"You and nobody else ought to tell that tale," Doc said. "Folks don't know if it's true or not, but they tell it all the time. Sooner or later some bastard is going to hear it and think he can make Adam tell where he hid it."

Turnbull did turn from the bar then, afraid his expression would give his feelings away. He was not only safe, but if Judy did regain her memory before Turnbull left town, the chances were that Ed Drumm or no one else would believe what she'd said after losing her memory this way.

It was the second piece of information that made him feel good. As he climbed the stairs, he told himself that they'd rob the store, then ride north to the Big J and relieve Adam Jones of his money. Ten or fifteen thousand dollars was enough to make a stop worthwhile.

They wouldn't have any trouble persuading Adam Jones to tell where he'd hidden his money. Jim Turnbull and his men were experts at the gentle art of persuasion.

Chapter XIV

Judy's headache gradually diminished through the following week, and although her bullet wound was painful, it was superficial and soon started to heal. In spite of her aches and pains, she did an enormous amount of work that week and never complained. Bud respected her for it, but still he had not made up his mind about her.

Dolan and Luke had no such trouble. Dolan was so much in love with Judy he was foolish. He spent every minute with her that he could, he helped her clean house, he saw to it that she always had an ample supply of wood, and he pumped water for her when she washed clothes or wanted to heat water to clean house.

Dolan never tried to touch her. She apparently sensed his shyness and often reached out and took his hand and held it, or gently laid a hand on his shoulder. Bud, watching her, knew that she was trying to encourage him, and he wondered how far she would go.

Luke spent no more time with Judy than he had had to, which meant he was in the house during meal time and he slept in his bed at night. During the rest of the time he was out on the range or was puttering around the barn and corral.

"Dolan needs her and he can have her," Luke told Bud. "She ain't my kind of woman, but she suits Dolan."

"How would you know what was your kind of woman?" Bud asked.

Luke shrugged. "I don't rightly know, but I'll find her and I'll know when I do," Luke said.

80

"You're in love with her just like Dolan is," Bud said. "Why don't you come right out and admit it?"

Luke scratched the back of his head and stared across the mesa toward the ridge tops to the west. Finally he said, "Hell's gonna pop the minute Pa gets home. You know it and I know it, but damned if Dolan does. I guess I can't face what's going to happen."

Luke shrugged his big shoulders again and turned back to Bud. "Hell, I ain't gonna run no race with Dolan for her. Like I said, he can have her." He studied Bud a moment, then asked. "You don't like her, do you?"

"I like her, all right," Bud said. "The house is clean for the first time I can remember, our clothes are washed and patched, and the meals we're getting are good, but I just ain't sure about her. She's after a place to live and she'll do anything to get it. She'd crawl into bed with Dolan today if he'd let her."

Luke laughed shortly. "Well, Dolan won't. Or if he did, he'd be so scared he couldn't do nothing. She'd better not give me the chance, though." He thought about it a moment, then he added, "I don't see nothing wrong with that, Bud. She's a worker, and that's the most important thing about a woman on a ranch."

"But damn it," Bud said sharply, "we don't know nothing about her. We don't know where she came from or how she happened to be here or anything else. She was running away from something, I guess, and got here on the mesa by accident, but what was she running from? The kid who was killed? Or whoever killed him?"

"I dunno," Luke said. "I sure dunno."

"Once she's got a place to stay permanent," Bud said, "she might not be such a worker."

That was the way it stood on the morning Adam Jones was due back in Hillcrest. Breakfast was a silent meal, Luke and Bud reluctant to face the day, and Dolan acting as if he didn't realize what was going to happen.

Judy acted as if she was not afraid of what would happen, but she had the excuse of not knowing Adam Jones, Bud thought. Dolan had no such excuse. He sat staring at Judy with a stupid, puppy-dog expression on his face which irritated Bud, but at the same time Bud real-

81

ized falling in love with the girl was good for Dolan. It would either kill him or make a man out of him.

When they finished eating, Luke pushed his chair back and asked, "You going to town to meet Pa, Bud?"

"I didn't figure on it," Bud answered. "You're the oldest, so it's your job."

"Doesn't he know his way home?" Judy asked in an outraged tone.

"He expects us to meet him," Luke said. "One of us anyway. Usually all three of us are standing beside the track when the train pulls in, but one of us will have to do it this time." He cleared his throat, and added, "You meet him, Bud. You're right about me being the oldest, so I'm telling you to meet him."

Bud grinned. "All right. Just one thing, though. When we get home, I want you and Dolan sitting in the front room and I want Judy back here in the kitchen making enough noise for Pa to know somebody's back here. I dunno how it'll work no more than the rest of you do, but it's my guess that it'll be better for us if it comes as a surprise. I won't tell him, and I'll try to head off anybody in town who starts telling him."

Judy sat very straight, her eyes moving from Dolan to Luke to Bud, and then she said scornfully, "I never in all my life heard of a situation like this before. Three big, grown-up men afraid of their father the way you three are. He must be some kind of a monster."

"There's some who say he is," Bud said.

He rose, took his hat off the peg near the back door, and left the house. Luke said, "You got no right to make any judgment like you just done till you meet pa. After that you'll know."

Luke left the house then. Suddenly contrite, Judy rose and walked around the table to Dolan. She put an arm on his shoulders and leaned down and kissed him. She said, "I don't want to leave here. You won't let your father kick me out, will you? I feel like this is home."

Dolan's face turned red. He sat frozen for several seconds, then he burst out, "No, I won't let him kick you out. No, by God, I won't."

She kissed him again. "I didn't think you would, Dolan," she said.

Bud reached town an hour before the train was due. He left his horse in the livery stable and went to the hotel bar first. He said to the bartender, "Jumbo, chances are Pa will come in here after a drink. If you mention that me and my brothers had a drink here the day he left, or that there's a girl staying with us, I'll fix that mug of yours so nobody can stand looking at it for a week."

"I ain't one to go looking for trouble," the bartender said. "It always comes soon enough with Adam anyhow."

Bud left the hotel and stepped into Abe Runkel's store. He said, "I look for Pa to get in on the noon train today. I don't know if he'll come in here for anything or not, but if he does, don't say nothing about the clothes we bought for the girl who's staying on the Big J or even that she's out there."

Runkel put his hand palm down on the counter and leaned forward, his face close to Bud's. He said in a low tone that pulsated with emotion, "there'll be all the trouble I can stand the minute Adam looks over his charge account when he comes in to pay which he always does after he sells his steers. I ain't one to hurry that trouble along."

He drew back and straightened up and took a long breath. He added, "You and your brothers had better be here to give me a hand when Adam finds out. He may kill me."

"He might at that," Bud said, and left the store.

He went to the depot to wait. As he paced nervously back and forth on the cinders beside the track, Ed Drumm came out of the depot and joined him. He asked, "Has your girl got her memory back yet?"

Bud shook his head. "She says not. I won't call her a liar, but I suspicion she remembers more'n she lets on."

The sheriff nodded. "I figgered so when I was talking to her. Doc told me about the shooting. The bullet hole didn't hurt her much?"

"She limped around on it," Bud answered, "and I reckon it hurt her all right, but she kept on working. We've got a clean house, Ed."

"What'll Adam say?"

"We wish we knew," Bud said glumly.

83

"It's a hell of a note for a man to live most of his lifetime," Drumm said, "and come to the place Adam is, where everybody who knows him is so damned afraid of him that he don't have a real friend in the world."

"It is for a fact," Bud agreed. "He'd never admit it, but I think he's a lonely man who would like to have some friends."

"Even one of his own boys," Drumm said.

Bud nodded. "Even one of his own boys."

"Well, if it gets to the place where you need me, just holler," Drumm said, and walked back into the depot.

The train rolled in a few minutes later, bell clanging and brakes squealing as it jerked to a stop. Adam Jones was the first to swing down from the smoker, a fresh cigar tucked between his teeth, his suitcase in his hand. Bud walked toward him, thinking that his father would never mention he had spent most of the week in Denver whorehouses and saloons and gambling halls, but Bud didn't doubt for a moment that that was the case.

"Well, where's the other two?" Adam boomed.

"They had work to do," Bud said, "so I came alone."

"That's a hell of a note," Adam said, plainly irritated. "I'll tell 'em when I see 'em that work ain't that important." He slapped Bud on the back. "I'm glad you're here. We'll get a drink and git to moving. We'll eat dinner when we get home."

Adam strode up the slope to the hotel, Bud half running to keep up. He glanced at his father, noting the network of red veins that showed on his face every time he went on a drinking spree. The incongruity of the situation struck Bud so hard that he almost laughed aloud.

Adam Jones worked very hard when he was home; he lived a Puritan life and demanded the same from his boys, but when he made a trip to Denver, he raised hell and propped it up with a chunk. Of course he never admitted it, but judging from the stories that filtered back to Hillcrest, Adam Jones made himself notorious every time he was in Denver.

Adam left his suitcase in the lobby of the hotel, saying he would pick it up next week when he brought a rig to town, then went into the bar. He said in a loud voice,

"Whisky, Jumbo, and none of your bellywash. Give the boy here a bottle of strawberry pop."

Bud's hands fisted at his sides, his pulse hammered in his forehead. He'd had his twenty-first birthday this week, but his father didn't know it. Bud was still "boy" to him, and Dolan and Luke would have been the same if they'd come to town with Bud.

"I don't want it, Jumbo," Bud said, and turned away.

Adam didn't seem to notice. He squinted thoughtfully at his drink for a moment, then said, "I've been to Denver, Jumbo. It's quite a city."

"I've been there," Jumbo said.

Adam lifted his glass and had his drink, then he set the glass back on the cherrywood bar with a bang. "Folks coming in yet for the fair?"

"A few," Jumbo said. "Mostly men with horses they figure on racing."

"Sure," Adam said, "they're the ones who get here first. Well, let's go home, boy. I sold my steers, Jumbo, so I'll come in the first of the week and settle up."

He strode out of the bar, slapping the batwings back with both hands and turned toward the livery stable. When he reached the archway, he called, "Saddle my horse, Polk. I've been gone for a week. I want to get back to the Big J and see how good the boys took care of things while I was gone."

The hostler winked at Bud as he turned into the stall that held Adam's horse. "Well, sir, they took care of things while you was gone, Adam. They sure did. I guess you've got a surprise coming."

"A surprise?" Adam asked. "What'd they do now?"

Bud had moved into the stall beside Polk and kicked him hard on the right shin just above the top of his boot. He said out of the corner of his mouth, "Shut up."

Polk muttered a curse and stood on one foot for a moment, surprised, then he said, "I reckon they'll have to tell you, Adam."

"What is it, Bud?" Adam asked.

"Nothing," Bud said. "Old Blabbermouth here sure has got the runs. We broke that big black gelding is all. Luke made a good ride and now that horse is tolerable gentle."

85

"I'd like to have seen it," Adam said. "You should of waited till I got home."

There was little talk between them as they rode home. Adam asked a few questions and Bud answered them and told him about the gullywasher they'd had the afternoon after Adam left. He mentioned the murder of the boy along the creek and that Ed Drumm had been out to see if any strangers had showed up on the mesa.

"I'm surprised that keg of lard would ride so far," Adam said in disgust. "We've got to get us a different sheriff next year."

When they reached the house, Bud reined up in front and said, "Let's leave the horses here right now, Pa. I'll take care of 'em a little later."

He stepped down and Adam, who had gone on past the house, turned and rode back. "Well now, I don't see no reason why we can't put the horses up . . ."

"Howdy, Pa," Luke called from the front porch. "Come on in. Dinner's ready."

Adam dismounted, growling something about leaving the horses. He strode up the path to the house, crossed the porch and went through the front door into the living room. Dolan was standing by the fireplace. He asked, "Have a good trip, Pa?"

"Sure did, boy," Adam said.

Bud and Dolan had followed him into the house. The clatter of dishes came to them from the kitchen. Adam scowled and looked at his three sons as if counting them to see which one was in the kitchen, then seemed to realize suddenly that they were all here in the front room.

Adam wheeled away from his boys and took long steps to the kitchen doorway. Judy was frying steak at the range. Now she turned and smiled and said, "Welcome home, Mr. Jones."

Adam stopped dead still in the doorway, his lips springing open. He began to sway back and forth like a stalk of wheat in a heavy wind, then reached up and gripped the casing to steady himself.

He took a long breath and said in a tone so low that Bud barely heard it, "My God, a woman, and in my house."

Chapter XV

ADAM remained in the doorway for several seconds, his breath sawing out of him into the silence, his hand gripping the casing so hard his fingers were white. Suddenly he released his grip and took three lurching steps to the nearest kitchen chair and sat down.

Adam's movement broke the spell that had paralyzed the others. Stepping forward, Bud said, "Pa, this is Judy Dunn. She's been keeping house for us. She was riding on the mesa and got throwed off her mare the day you went to Denver. We found her knocked out and lying on the ground when we rode home."

"She's worked hard for us all week," Dolan said, "fixing up our clothes and cleaning house and such."

"She's a hell of a good cook, too," Luke added. "What we've been eating this week ain't much like Dolan's cooking."

Adam acted as if he didn't hear. He continued to stare at Judy as spittle ran down the corners of his mouth. He wiped it off with a sleeve, and just as Judy started to say she was glad to see him, he bawled, "Get out of my house. Our clothes were all right and we could eat Dolan's cooking and the house wasn't dirty. We don't need no woman here. We ain't had a woman here since the boys' ma walked out on us and we ain't having you here, neither."

Frightened by his threatening tone, Judy backed up until she bumped against the range. She whirled and began forking steak from the frying pan into a platter,

87

then set the platter in the warming oven. Luke and Bud exchanged glances. Bud said softly, "It's your deal this time. You're still the oldest."

Luke nodded, his lips pressed so tightly together they became a thin, white line. He moved past Bud and stood in front of Adam. He said, "You're calling for a show-down, Pa, so you're gonna get it. We like having a woman in the house. We like what she does."

"I'll bet you do." Adam got to his feet and ran a hand across his mouth. "Yes, sir, I'll bet you've all had one hell of a good time sleeping with her since I left. Took turns, didn't you? All women are whores. You've heard me say that a dozen times. Look at what your ma did. Well, I sure ain't standing for it in my house. Now git her out of here."

"If you wasn't my father," Luke said, "I'd bust your dirty, lying mouth all over your front teeth. None of us have laid a hand on her. She ain't offered no bed space to none of us, neither."

"We're pulling out, Pa," Bud said. "Tell him the rest of it, Luke."

"You bet we're pulling out," Luke said. "We're taking our saddles and guns and horses. You're paying regular wages to me and Dolan for every month we've worked here since we were twenty-one. We'd have left before, but we wanted to stay together, and we figured Bud had to stay till he was twenty-one."

"Now I am," Bud said. "We weren't sure we'd leave if you were willing to let Judy stay, but you ain't, so we're riding out today and we're taking Judy with us."

Adam still acted as if he heard nothing they had said. He started toward Judy, saying, "You must be deaf, girl. I told you to git out, but you ain't done it, so now I'm gonna throw you out of the house on your butt."

Luke and Bud closed in on him, moving swiftly to his sides, their guns in their hands. They jammed the muzzles into his ribs hard, Luke saying, "You lay a hand on Judy and you're a dead man."

"We ain't worrying about Ed Drumm arresting us for murder, neither," Bud said. "I talked to him this morning. He said to call him if we had any trouble."

Dolan had rushed into the front room. Now he ran

back into the kitchen carrying the shotgun he had snatched off the antler rack near the front door. He jammed the muzzle into the small of Adam's back, screaming, "You hurt Judy and by God, I'll blow your backbone apart."

He was almost hysterical, sweat running down his cheeks and converging on his chin and dripping off in tiny drops. Bud, glancing at him, realized that he was close to losing control of himself. He was never given to violence, and Bud knew that by nature Dolan was the gentlest and most compassionate of the three of them, but at this moment he was almost a madman.

"Easy, Dolan," Bud said, "let me and Luke handle this."

Slowly he transferred his revolver from his right to his left hand, then reached out with his right hand and, gripping the barrel of the shotgun, pulled it toward him so the buckshot would not slam into Adam's back if the shotgun was fired.

Dolan backed away, lowering the barrel toward the floor. Judy came quickly to him from the stove and put an arm around him. "Let's sit down, Dolan," she said. "We need to talk awhile."

"I ain't letting you go," he said. "I ain't letting Pa talk that way about you, neither."

"He didn't really mean it," Judy said. "He was just surprised to find me here."

"Oh, he meant it, all right," Dolan said. "He's a mean son-of-a-bitch. We told you, didn't we?"

"Yes, you told me," Judy said. "Now come over here and sit down. I'll sit beside you."

He let her take his arm and lead him to a chair on the other side of the table. He sat down and held the shotgun across his lap as Judy pulled up a chair and sat down beside him. Bud had holstered his gun and stepped away from Adam.

"You know how close you came to getting shot just now?" Bud asked in a low tone.

Adam's face held a strange expression, an expression Bud had never seen there before. He guessed it was one of fear, although he had never thought Adam was capable of feeling fear. The color of the skin of his face had turned to a sort of bilious green and his eyes were glazed. Beads of sweat had popped out all over his face and he was actually trembling, something else Bud had never thought he would see.

"I know," Adam whispered. "Have you all been eating loco weed? Or has this woman got you all hypnotized?"

"Neither one," Luke answered. "We've talked it over a lot of times and planned to leave as soon as Bud was twenty-one, but I guess it took your threats about hurting Judy that finally done it. We've had to work our tails off for you since we were little and you've beaten us sometimes until we hurt for a week afterwards, but that's all over with. We took it too long."

"That's right," Bud said. "Now we're leaving and you can hire help to run the Big J. All we want are the wages Luke and Dolan have coming."

Adam wiped his face with his sleeve again and turned to Dolan. He said, "I never figured you, boy. I don't now. I never have punished you like I done the others. What's got into you?"

Dolan was over his hysteria now. He was holding Judy's hand. He glanced at her, then slowly brought his gaze to Adam's face as he said, "That's right, but I've seen you beat Luke and Bud and I always wondered when I was going to get it as bad as they did. Now you were going to do to Judy what you'd done to them. You put your dirty tongue on her."

He paused, his lips curling in contempt, then he added, "I've never been much of a man the way you look at it, but I reckon I am now. I could have killed you just as easy as I would have shot a coyote, and there ain't a man in this county who would have said I done wrong."

Adam stumbled back to the chair where he had been sitting and sat down again. He moistened his lips with the tip of his tongue, then he said, "I guess this is a bad dream. A real bad dream. I don't believe it's happening. It couldn't be."

"It's happening, all right," Luke said. "You made it happen. Now if you'll get the wages we've got coming, we'll get out of here and you can run the Big J without any woman on the place just as long as you want to."

Adam shook his head. "I don't want to do that. You boys have been fine help. I . . . well, maybe I ain't been as good to you as I should of been." He swallowed, and went on, "Maybe you're running a bluff on me, but I ain't gonna call it if you are. I promise everything will be different from now on if you'll stay. I'll even pay you wages. Regular wages."

"We've been treated like little kids long enough," Bud said, exasperated. "You had your chance, but you couldn't change. I don't believe you will now, so go get the dinero we're asking for."

Still Adam sat there, not moving, his gaze turning from one to the other. He said finally, "I'll let you call any tune you want to from now on. The girl can stay. It ain't easy for me to admit I've been wrong, but I'll say it now if that's what you want to hear. I can't let you go. You're all I've got, all I've ever had since your ma left me."

Adam choked up and bowed his head. Bud, staring at him, could not believe this was happening. This, too, must be some kind of dream, or so it seemed, just as a moment before Adam could not believe that what was happening was real.

Bud had always supposed his father hated all three of them. He could not remember Adam ever showing any affection or appreciation for the work they had done. Now, suddenly and unexpectedly, his father was a broken man.

Dolan rose, the shotgun still in his hands. "I don't believe anything will change, but I vote to try it." He faced Luke. "I guess Pa knows by this time how we feel and what will happen if he tries setting the clock back."

Bud and Luke looked at each other, surprised that Dolan would say this, and even more surprised at Adam. Slowly Luke nodded and Bud said reluctantly, "All right, Pa, we'll give it a try, but the minute you go back on your word, we're pulling out like we said. You're getting Luke's and Dolan's wages, and you're paying for what we bought at the store for Judy without cussing us for buying it. Savvy?"

Adam nodded, his head still bowed. Judy jumped up and, running to the range, opened the oven and jerked out a pan of biscuits. "I forgot all about them," she said. "They're pretty brown, but we can eat them. Let's have dinner before everything is completely spoiled."

"You go ahead and eat," Adam said. "I ain't hungry."

He got up and walked to the back door and on across the porch, reeling like a drunk man. Bud said, "I didn't think anything could hit like this."

"We should have done it a long time before," Luke said. "I guess we're cowards."

"Not now we ain't," Dolan said as he pulled his chair up to the table. "I feel ten feet tall. I never thought I could kill a man, but now I know I can."

Bud crossed the kitchen to the back door and looked out. He called, "Come here, all of you."

They followed him and looked past him at Adam who had started toward the corral, but he hadn't gone more than thirty feet. He was bent over, a very sick man.

They turned away, Judy whispering, "I'm to blame for this. I'm sorry."

"Don't be," Bud said harshly. "It's like Luke and me were saying once. We wouldn't have had the guts to face Pa without you being here."

"That's right," Dolan said. "You've changed our lives more'n you'll ever know, Judy."

She nodded and smiled as if pleased. "Then I'm glad," she said. "I'll work hard for all three of you. I promise." She turned to Dolan and put an arm around him and hugged him. "And for you most of all."

Bud, looking at Dolan's face, knew that Adam had been right about one thing. She did have Dolan hypnotized.

Chapter XVI

JIM TURNBULL was lucky. He slept in his bed in his hotel room and ate most of his meals in the hotel dining room and did most of his drinking in the hotel bar. Ed Drumm ignored him except to speak to him curtly when they met or give him a bare, half-inch nod.

Turnbull was indeed lucky and he was very much aware of it. He didn't know what Judy Dunn's motives were, but she hadn't talked. He was dead sure of that or Drumm would have been after him before this. He grew more confident as each day passed. If she hadn't talked by this time, she wasn't likely to talk at all. Or, if her memory was still gone, there was no reason to think it would suddenly return now.

He dropped into the store several times and bought smoking tobacco and shells for his Colt and his 30-30. He casually studied the interior of the building each time until he could draw it from memory. Cold Dan Summers was the expert on safes, but Turnbull had been with him enough times when Summers had opened safes to identify the ones that would be stubborn and he was confident this safe would give Summers no trouble at all.

People in large numbers drifted into town for the fair. The ones who brought horses to race were the first and therefore were the ones who rented rooms. The hotel refused to take reservations and went on the basis that whoever got there first got rooms. By the middle of the week the hotel was full, the dining room and bar echoed with horse talk; bets were made and later recorded in Abe Runkel's store.

The excitement and tension grew with each passing day, and Turnbull was caught up in it. He made a few small bets, thinking that he was less likely to be noticed if he did what everybody else was doing. Several times when he was in Runkel's store, men came in with bags of money and left them in the safe. Twice Turnbull caught a glimpse of the interior. Both times his pulse began to pound. The safe was crammed with canvas money sacks, some apparently filled with currency and some bulging with coins.

Turnbull's men were slower arriving in Hillcrest than he had expected. Two days before the fair started, Cold Dan Summers appeared in the hotel bar. Turnbull saw him, but neither gave any sign that he recognized the other. The next day just before noon, Pancho Juarez and Slick Ed Schuster rode in, and late that afternoon Lucky Dick Norton and Pete Keller made their appearance. That was the outfit, five men, or six with Turnbull, every one an expert at murder and assorted forms of robbery.

Turnbull realized that he could never round up another gang as efficient as this one; he also realized that he could and would be replaced as leader any time his plans failed. It took a good haul to satisfy six greedy men. There had been times when they hadn't been satisfied. If the contents of Abe Runkel's safe was below expectation, he was in trouble.

As soon as he finished supper that evening, he went to his room, leaving his door unlocked. The six men had worked together long enough to know what to do without specific instructions. A glance at the register on the clerk's desk would tell his men his room number. The trick was for his men to look like ordinary cowboys who were in town for the fair.

By eight o'clock that night the five men had slipped into Turnbull's room. Turnbull had prepared two maps, one of the interior of the store, the other of the surrounding country with the Big J clearly marked.

He passed the map of the store around first and waited while each man examined it. Cold Dan Summers was the last to see it. One quick glance satisfied him and he handed it back to Turnbull.

94

"No trouble," Summers said. "I've been in the store three times since I got to town. I'll have that safe open in sixty seconds. The store is the same as you find in any two-bit cowtown. Even smells the same."

"I didn't think you'd have any trouble," Turnbull said.

"Got any idea how much is in the safe?" Lucky Dick Norton asked.

"I didn't count it," Turnbull said testily, "but I've had a look at the inside when it was open to put more dinero in, and it's chock-full. You be sure you've got the sacks, Pancho." He nodded at Juarez. "We won't be taking the dinero out of that store in our pockets."

"*Si,*" Juarez said. "I've got 'em."

"Who stays in the store while the races are being run?" Slick Ed Schuster asked.

"Just the owner, Abe Runkel," Turnbull said, "as far as I know anyhow. Nobody thinks about the safe being robbed. I mentioned it one time and the fellow I was talking to said nobody had better try it. If they catch up with us, it'll be a rope."

Cold Dan Summers snickered. "They won't. Easy as taking candy from a baby, as the man says."

"Now take a careful look at this map," Turnbull said as he handed the second one to Pete Keller. "I've been here about two weeks pretending to be a horse rancher looking for a spread. I've ridden all over the country and I've looked at twelve, fifteen ranches. The only one I'm interested in is the Big J. It's all by itself on a mesa and off the beaten path."

They looked at each other, frowned, and shuffled their feet. Turnbull knew what they were thinking. The plan was to rob the store safe and he was coming up with something in addition. This was the first time the plan had ever been changed at the last minute, if that was what Turnbull had in mind and all five of them were preparing to fight him on his idea no matter how good it was.

He didn't say anything more until the second map had gone the rounds. After Cold Dan Summers had examined it and tossed it on the bed, Turnbull asked, "Any of you come in from the north."

They shook their heads. Turnbull went on, "I did. I

think it's the one way out of this country they'd never think of us taking. My plan is for us to start down the river, then swing back north as soon as we're out of sight from town. It'll take 'em a while to organize a posse. When they do, we'll be a long ways up Banner Creek. That's the main road north. By the time they get around to thinking we went up Banner Creek, we'll be off of it and on the mesa."

They were still looking at each other and not liking anything he said worth a damn. He thought that if any of them bucked him openly, it would be Cold Dan Summers, and he was right.

"It's always been our plan to break up and ride in different directions," Summers said. "I came up the river and I rode alone. I'm leaving the same way."

"All right," Turnbull said, "that sure as hell is your privilege, but I ain't done." He nodded at Lucky Dick Norton. "You asked how much was in the store safe. My guess is that it'll be between $50,000 and $100,000."

He turned to Summers. "You'd better hear the rest of this. The Big J is a dividend we hadn't counted on. It belongs to a man named Adam Jones. He's the kind of gent you hear about, but you don't often see. He's as tight as the hide on a bull. He's mean and ornery as hell, but he's got a good spread and three sons who work for him for nothing. He don't like banks, so he's got all his savings hid around his house. I don't know where, but we'll find it."

For a long moment nobody said a word, then Slick Ed Schuster shook his head, muttering, "Not me. You say there's four men on that spread. They'd cut us to pieces."

Then Cold Dan Summers surprised Turnbull. He said, "I don't think so, Ed. We can handle 'em. If Jones has his dinero hid on his place, we'll get it."

Schuster threw up his hands. "All right, I'll go along. You change horses might damn fast, Dan."

Summers laughed softly. "There's only one thing that makes me change horses on a deal like this and that's money. I'm greedy. If you ain't, I don't know why you're here in this game." He pinned his gaze on Turnbull. "It had better be there, Jim."

"All I can tell you is what I hear," Turnbull said, "and everything I've heard adds up to the same thing. It's there, all right." He looked at the men in front of him, trying to measure their feelings. As far as he could tell, they were satisfied. "If there's no questions, I guess that's about it. Noon tomorrow."

"Where do we get together next time?" Pete Keller asked.

"Cheyenne in two weeks," Turnbull said. "Dyer's Hotel. I got wind of a little burg north of Cheyenne that's got a bank with enough dinero to make it worth hitting."

They nodded, then Norton asked, "Where's the woman who was riding with you? Judy something or other?"

"Judy Dunn," Turnbull answered sourly. "She left me."

"The hell," Summers said, surprised. "I thought you were a man who always left them before they left you."

"I always have been," Turnbull said shortly.

"And the Kid?" Schuster asked. "The idiot?"

"He wasn't an idiot," Turnbull snapped.

"He was close to it," Schuster said. "What happened to him?"

"He's dead," Turnbull said.

"Good riddance," Summers muttered, and turned to the door.

He stepped into the hall, made a quick motion to the others to indicate that all was clear, then strode toward the head of the stairs. A moment later they were all out of the room, the door was shut, and Jim Turnbull dropped on his bed, suddenly tired. He had been in this game long enough, too long. He had money banked in Denver, and with what he'd get out of the robbery tomorrow, he'd have enough to live in style in Mexico. He had no intention of showing up in Cheyenne in two weeks. He'd head for Denver, get his money out of the bank, and ride to Chihuahua.

Then he thought about Judy and what Cold Dan Summers had said, and a flood of bitterness swept through him. His pride was hurt and so was his reputation. He shouldn't have admitted she had left him. It had popped out before he'd thought about what he was saying.

Well, there would be some shots fired tomorrow while they were finding Adam Jones's money. Before it was over, Judy would pay for what she had done to him, pay with her life.

Chapter XVII

THE WEEK was hell for Judy Dunn for two reasons. One was the hostility that was barely skin deep between Adam Jones and his boys. Adam went on living much the way he always had, giving orders and acting as if he would stand for no arguments from anybody.

The boys obeyed his orders in sullen silence, but they made no effort to hide their feelings for him. Even at meal time the air crackled with suppressed violence, and Judy sensed that it would take very little to bring the violence into the open.

Dolan showed the greatest change. Judy knew that by nature he was a very gentle and mild man, but now he was never far from his shotgun. He would use it if circumstances demanded it. Judy had no doubt of that. Before the week was over, she had the feeling she was actually living a hideous nightmare and could not wake up.

The second reason was even harder to live with because it kept Judy awake at night with the nagging knowledge that time was running out for her. She alone, except for Turnbull and his gang, knew about the plan to rob the store.

Judy didn't think that Adam or any of the boys had money in Runkel's safe. She knew the boys didn't as soon as she thought about it. They didn't have any money unless Adam had paid Luke and Dolan the wages they had coming. She didn't think he had or she would have heard about it. In any case, they would not have taken it to town.

No, it wasn't so much the money that would be lost. It was the lives that would be taken and Judy would blame herself for the deaths as long as she lived. Turnbull liked to kill. He'd proved it by shooting the Kid. Cold Dan Summers was the same way. She didn't know about the other four, but she guessed all of them had the same bloody appetite.

Abe Runkel certainly would be murdered. Anyone else who happened to be in the store at the wrong time would be killed because Turnbull believed that if there wasn't anyone to swear he had actually witnessed the robbery there would be no convictions.

Judy had promised herself all week that she would tell about the robbery scheme, but somehow the right moment never came. When they ate supper that evening, she knew she could not keep silent any longer. It would be too late if she did.

"I've got something to tell all of you," Judy said as they finished their apple pie. "It's not easy, but I can't put it off any longer."

"It can wait, Judy," Adam said. "I've got something to say first."

"Why don't you clean up the dishes?" Bud asked. "We'll wait for you in the other room."

She sighed with relief, thankful for even this short reprieve. She said, "I guess it would be better."

She hurried with the dishes. Dolan brought in an armload of wood, then laid the shotgun across the table. He picked up a dishcloth and started drying dishes. Presently he said in a worried tone, "I don't know what pa's aiming to say, but it ain't gonna be good. You'd best be ready for anything."

"Aren't you worried about what I'm going to say?" she asked.

"No." He looked at her a moment and shook his head. "You don't know what it's meant to me to have you here. I've read about love, but I never knew what it was like till you came. I guess you've known all the time that I'm in love with you, but I can't ask you to marry me until I've got a job and proved to myself I can get a job and hold it."

"Oh, Dolan," she said softly. "Don't say that. I would

100

never hold back because you don't have a job, but I couldn't marry you if you asked me. I'm not what you think I am. After I tell you, you won't want to marry me."

"Hogwash," he said. "You couldn't tell me anything that would change my mind about wanting to marry you. I don't care what you have been or what you've done. I love you. That's all that's important, but I've got to prove I can support you before I'll ask you to marry me. I haven't proved it yet. I've changed some since you came, but I won't know how much until the chips are down."

"Honey, you're a different man than you were two weeks ago. I know. I've seen you change." She swallowed and added, "Bud has seen it, too. He and Luke are proud of you."

Quickly he picked up a plate and turned away, not wanting her to see the tears than ran down his cheeks. She carried the dishpan to the back porch and threw the dish water into the yard. She returned and put the dishes away that Dolan had dried, then found another dishcloth and helped until they were finished. Dolan picked up the shotgun and went into the front room. Judy followed a moment later.

Before Judy could open her mouth, Adam said in his commanding voice. "All right, I'll tell you what I've decided to do. It's damned good to have a woman in the house. I don't admit very often that I've been wrong, but I'll admit it this time. The grub is better than you used to cook, Dolan."

Adam nodded at Dolan who had leaned his shotgun against the wall and now stood just inside the door that opened into the kitchen. Judy sat down on the couch. Bud and Luke were seated near the fireplace. Adam was sitting in his rocking chair near the claw-footed oak stand in the center of the room.

Dolan stared sullenly at his father, not returning even a hint of Adam's smile. Bud and Luke, too, were somber as Adam's gaze turned to them. Judy thought: "He's trying to be friendly. He still doesn't know it's too late."

"Of course we can't go on this way," Adam said, "a single woman living in a house with four men. We can't have the neighbors gossiping about us."

Judy shot a glance at Bud and saw that he was having trouble holding back his laughter. He was the only one in the family who had a real sense of humor, Judy had discovered. Dolan was too intense and Luke was too much like his father to laugh spontaneously the way Bud did.

She knew what was amusing Bud, although she found it more frightening than amusing. Adam Jones had never worried about the neighbors gossiping before in his life, but he did now because he had found a way to use it for his own selfish purposes. Judy didn't know yet what his purpose was, but she was dead sure it was selfish. She didn't think Adam Jones ever had any other kind of thought.

Adam cleared his throat and went on, "I've decided that the only thing we can do is for me to marry Judy and then she'll be here to cook for us and . . .

"No," Judy said, realizing she had plenty of reason to be frightened and she had to stop Adam immediately. Dolan was reaching for his shotgun and Luke and Bud were on their feet. "I won't marry you, Mr. Jones. I've got to tell you about me. I remembered several days ago how I happened to be here, but I've put off telling you. Now I'm going to tell you and you won't want to marry me after I do."

"Don't Judy," Bud said. "You don't have to tell us anything."

"Yes, I do, Bud," she said doggedly. "You'll know why in a minute. I won't tell you about my home in Kansas except that it was unbearable. The man who calls himself Jim Turnbull rode into our community and stayed for several weeks. He changes his name so often that he admits he has to look at his hatband every once in a while to remember what he's calling himself right then. He never did tell me what his real name was.

"Anyhow, he was calling himself Turnbull when I met him and he's still using that name. I think he would have changed it when he went into Hillcrest if he had guessed I was leaving him, but he didn't know that then.

"You see, I thought he was a good man and would take care of me and marry me, but I was never so wrong about anything. I ran away from home with him, and after I left, I found out he was an outlaw who had a gang that worked with him robbing banks. By that time I couldn't go back. I guess he had come to our community to hide out. I know he didn't have any business there and he didn't look for a job. The boy who was killed rode with us. I never heard his name. He was just called the Kid."

She stopped and wiped her eyes, then hurried on before she lost her nerve. "I soon found out that living with Turnbull was as bad as my home had been, or worse. I tried to get away from him, but I didn't make it until we camped on Banner Creek and he rode into town. That was when I hit the Kid with a limb and came up here on the mesa and was thrown by my horse."

She swallowed, her gaze on the floor. She was afraid to look at any of them. This was the place where she wanted to stay. For the first time in her life she felt loved. She was appreciated. She could give something that was needed in return for what she received, but now she sensed they . . . all of them . . . were backing away from her because she was admitting the kind of woman she was.

"It must have been Turnbull who tried to kill me the afternoon the doctor and his wife were here," she went on. "It must have been Turnbull who killed the Kid, too. He was probably mad because the Kid let me get away. He doesn't care anything about me. It's just that I know what his plans are and that makes me dangerous to him."

She looked at Dolan then and could not believe what she saw in his face. Compassion was there and love, and he wanted her to know that. Suddenly she knew that he really had meant what he'd said about not caring what she had done or what she had been.

"I don't know the details of their plan," she said. "All I know is that Turnbull and his men plan to rob Runkel's store tomorrow at noon while everybody is at the race-track," she said, her gaze on Dolan's face because she could not bring herself to look at any of the others. "The safe will be filled with money the people have bet on the races. I guess you know more about that than I do.

"Turnbull wouldn't have planned this if they hadn't heard there was a lot of money. I don't know what they plan to do after the robbery. Usually they break up and

103

ride in opposite directions, but Turnbull knows I'm here and I can identify him. He might try again to kill me before he leaves the country. I had to tell you so you could warn the sheriff. Maybe he can stop the robbery."

"Sure, we'll tell him," Bud said. "He'll stop it, all right. Don't worry any more about it."

Adam was on his feet now, staring down at the girl. He said in a righteous tone, "You're right about no one wanting to marry you after hearing what you had to say. It's just like I've always told my boys. Every woman is a whore and you're as bad as any of them. You admit you left home to live with an outlaw and traipse around all over the country living with him . . ."

Dolan lunged at his father, shouting, "You damned old hypocrite." He hit Adam as hard as he could with an upswinging fist to the point of the big man's jaw. Adam's head jerked back, but Dolan wasn't strong enough to hurt his father. Adam raised an open palm and slapped Dolan on the side of the face, a powerful blow that sent him sprawling.

Judy cried out. She jumped and hit Adam a stinging blow on the side of his head. "You're an animal," she screamed. "No wonder everybody hates you."

Dolan scrambled to his feet and grabbed his shotgun away from the wall as Adam knocked Judy back onto the couch. Her head hit the wall and her feet flew up as Adam whirled toward Dolan, his right hand darting downward to the butt of his gun.

Luke and Bud had not expected anything like this to happen and they were slow, but now they were on Adam, each grabbing an arm as Bud yelled, "No, Dolan, no. Damn it, put that scattergun down."

"Get away," Dolan shouted. "I'm going to kill the bastard. You heard what he said to Judy. Now get away."

Judy bounced back off the couch and ran to Dolan and gripped his arms. She stood in front of him, saying softly, "No, Dolan, no. If you do love me, don't kill him. I want to marry you if you'll still have me after what I've told you, but not if you kill your father."

"Of course I still want to marry you." Dolan glared at Adam, his face red, his pulse pounding in his forehead. He cocked the shotgun, the barrel half-raised. "I ain't

104

standing still while Pa talks that way about you, Judy. I won't put up with it."

Adam had been wrestled halfway back across the room. Luke had managed to twist his revolver out of his grip. Bud said, "You've fixed it now so none of us can stay, but I reckon we've got to wait until we know whether Turnbull is going to try to kill Judy. Now are you gonna behave, Dolan?"

"Yeah, if he can keep his dirty tongue off Judy," Dolan said.

Bud turned to his father, who nodded. There would be peace for a moment, Judy thought, and that was about as long as it would last.

Chapter XVIII

ADAM rose and stomped out of the house without a word. Luke whistled softly and said in a low tone, "Well, by God, what do you think of Pa wanting to marry Judy after all the talking he's done about women?"

"He knew a good thing when he saw it," Bud said, "and then changed his mind. I guess he didn't want her very bad. Not like Dolan does."

Judy sat hunched forward on the couch, her head bowed. She was crying softly. Dolan sat down beside her and, putting an arm around her, pulled her to him. "It's all right, Judy. Everything's going to be all right." He looked at Bud. "It is, ain't it?"

"Sure, it is," Bud said. "Soon as it's daylight, I'll ride into town and tell Ed Drumm about Turnbull. I thought about riding in tonight, but Ed would be in bed and there's nothing he can do till morning anyhow."

"That's right," Luke agreed. "I think one of us had better stay up all night. We'll tell Pa we're afraid Turnbull might show up before morning, but Pa's the one I'm afraid of."

"If he tries getting into bed with Judy . . . ," Dolan began.

"We won't let him," Bud said. "He won't try it if one of us is sitting up."

Judy straightened and pulled away from Dolan's arm. "I'm sorry about all the trouble I'm causing," she said.

"You haven't caused any trouble," Dolan told her. "Don't talk that way."

"He's right, Judy," Bud said. "You've showed us how people ought to live instead of wallowing around in their own dirt the way we have for years. We're going to get that money from Pa tomorrow, then we'll head down the river. Maybe we'll go to Grand Junction. Luke and me will find jobs. I don't know what we'll do with you, Dolan, but you're going to get some schooling."

"I'll look funny in the third grade," Dolan said, "and that's about where I belong."

"We'll find a way," Luke said. "If we wasn't so damned ignorant, we'd know now what to do. Might be you'll have to go to Denver." Then he grinned. "Dolan, has Judy been slipping you some raw meat?"

"No. Why?"

"You used to be scared of your shadow and you never had a mean thought in your noggin," Luke said, "but since Judy got here, you've been toting that scattergun around and growling as mean as a sore-toed grizzly."

"He ain't just been growling," Bud said. "He'd have used that scattergun."

Dolan wiped his face with a sleeve and shook his head. "I don't exactly know what's got into me, but when I think that something might happen to Judy . . . I mean, that I might lose her, I get a funny feeling in my belly like maybe I'd swallowed a rock and it hadn't digested. Just seems like I've got to prove I can take care of her."

"After what I told you . . . ," Judy began.

"I said it wouldn't make any difference what you'd been or what you'd done," Dolan interrupted.

"Then don't wait to prove anything to anybody," Judy said. "Let's get married as soon as we leave here."

Bud nodded. "That's what I say. Now you go to bed, Judy. Luke, you'd better stay downstairs the first part of the night. I'll take the last part. I'll cook my own breakfast and be on my way to town by sunup."

After Judy had disappeared into her room and Dolan had gone upstairs, Luke said, "I reckon we'd better let Dolan sleep. We'll split the night, just you'n me."

"That's what I was going to say," Bud said.

"I sure don't savvy what's happened to Dolan," Luke said. "Judy's coming made him grow up in a hurry, but two weeks ago I would have said it wasn't possible for

107

him to do the things he's been doing. He really would have blowed Pa's head off if we hadn't butted in."

"Did it ever strike you that we never let Dolan grow up?" Bud said. "I've been the one who sassed Pa and kept getting into trouble, but Dolan held back, so we got to looking out for him. Now he's got to start looking after somebody else."

"He'll do it, too," Luke said. "Well, go on to bed. I'll call you about midnight."

Adam had not come back into the house when Bud dropped off to sleep. It seemed only a minute that Luke was shaking him awake. Bud sat up and pulled on his boots. He asked, "Pa come in yet?"

"No."

"I don't like it," Bud said. "I'll get you up before I ride out in the morning."

"He may be back before then," Luke said.

Bud was eating breakfast by lamplight when Adam came back into the house, his face gaunt and cut by deep lines Bud had never seen there before. "You want a cup of coffee?" Bud asked.

Adam nodded. Bud rose, poured a cup of coffee and set it in front of his father. Adam stared at the steaming brown liquid and then raised his head to look at Bud. "Is it too late to get you boys to change your mind about leaving? I'll do anything to keep you. Of course I didn't know then what she was."

"It's too late," Bud said.

He didn't want to talk about it and he didn't want to listen to his father beg him and his brothers to stay on the Big J. For the first time in his memory, Bud had the feeling that Adam Jones was a beaten man. He saw agony in his father's big, sun-blackened face, the agony of a man who could not face the truth. Adam Jones was a smart man, and Bud found it hard to understand how he could have failed to see what he was bringing on himself all these years.

Adam leaned forward, his big hands palm down on the table. "You're the youngest, but you're the leader. I've knowed that all the time since you were a little shaver, and I guess that was why I've been so hard on you. I tried my damnedest to make you knuckle under and you never would no matter what I done to you. .Now I'm sorry. I'd like to know that it ain't too late. Like I said, I'll do anything to get you to stay. If you do, the others will, too."

Bud drank the rest of his coffee and set the cup down. His father was begging. It was in his tone of voice, in the expression on his face, the old, familiar arrogance drained out of it. He wasn't the same man Bud had known for twenty-one years. He told himself that he would have respected Adam Jones more if he had remained the domineering bastard he had been all through the time Bud was growing up.

"I told you it was too late," Bud said. "We shouldn't have stayed this week. We figured it wouldn't work, but you wanted one more chance. You had it, Pa. If we stayed and gave you still another chance, it would end up the same way. We're going to live our own lives, and you can go on living yours the way you want to live it."

He left the kitchen and climbed the stairs. He shook Luke awake and said, "Pa's back. He's still after us to stay. Don't let him soft soap you into promising anything. We're leaving in the morning."

Luke rubbed his eyes as he swung his feet to the floor. "You bet we are."

Bud went back downstairs and out through the front door. Adam was still sitting at the kitchen table. Bud saddled his horse and rode south across the mesa, then turned west and took the narrow road down the sharp slope to Banner Creek.

He could not get over the changes Judy Dunn had brought to all of them in the two weeks she had been here. The final break with Adam would have come sooner or later, but it would not have been as sharp and complete as it was if Judy had not come to the Big J. And Dolan?

Bud smiled when he thought about Dolan. He guessed that it proved you could grow up with a brother and never really know him. Maybe he should have asked Luke to go to town this morning. He wasn't sure Luke could handle Dolan if Adam insulted Judy again.

He reached Hillcrest in mid-morning and found Main Street deserted. The races started at ten and ran until one, then there was a two-hour break with the afternoon races going from three until six. As he reined up in front of Ed Drumm's office, he heard a roar from the track. A race had just been finished, he thought. A few had won and a lot more had lost.

He told himself as he had many times that someday he would watch the races. Adam had often gone to them, but there had always been too much work for his sons to allow them to leave the ranch. It was another of the long list of abuses that Adam must be remembering and perhaps regretting.

Bud had been afraid Drumm would be at the race track, but he was relieved to find the sheriff sitting behind his desk. He nodded at Bud when he saw who had come in, and said, "I'm guessing your girl boarder suddenly remembered some things she had forgotten."

"You're right," Bud said, surprised. "How did you know?"

"I've been waiting," Drumm said sourly, "just hoping she'd decide to open up. The day I was out there I was damned sure she knew more than she let on, but she was too scared to talk, or else she didn't want to implicate herself. Then when she got shot that afternoon, I figured she'd be more scared than ever."

"She was," Bud admitted. "Last night she told it all. She had been wanting to tell it before, but couldn't bring herself to do it." He told Drumm what Judy had said, and added, "I promised her I'd get word to you and you'd stop it."

"I'll stop it, all right," Drumm said, "but if for any reason they back down, we won't get 'em. I don't have any proof that Turnbull killed the boy, and I can't hold him just on the girl's say so. I've gone through my reward dodgers a dozen times, and if he's wanted, I don't have any notice of it."

He slammed a hand against the top of his desk. "I've been watching that son of a bitch of a Turnbull every day since he rode into town. Or since he found the boy's body anyhow. I had a hunch he wasn't what he said he was, but he's never done a thing I could nail him for and I never see him with anyone else. He just rides around looking for a horse ranch, he says."

110

"You figured it wouldn't be him that killed the Kid," Bud said. "Not after he found the body."

"That's what I said," Drumm admitted, "but I didn't mean it. I figured the girl might go back to him after she got over her fall, but from what you say, she never planned to. I just didn't want him thinking I suspected him of anything. He's a slick one, all right. Finding the body and reporting it is just what you'd expect a man like that to do, but that ain't evidence." He rose. "Thanks for coming in, Bud. I've got to round up some men. We'll be ready for 'em."

Bud went back to his horse and watched Drumm hurry down a side street toward the race track. He wished he could stay and see what happened, but he knew he couldn't. He did not believe Turnbull would show up at the Big J regardless of what happened here, but now he wished he'd mentioned it to Drumm just on the off chance Turnbull did try to kill Judy.

He could leave a note on the sheriff's desk, then decided not. He was imagining more trouble, he told himself. It didn't make any sense that a gang of outlaws like Jim Turnbull and his men would stop on their way out of the country after a holdup just to murder a girl. No, once Turnbull and his men started to leave, they'd burn the breeze getting out of the country. Besides, they'd be dead or in jail. Either way, they wouldn't turn up at the Big J.

Bud mounted and rode back, more concerned about his father and Dolan than he was about Jim Turnbull. It might be smart to pull out this afternoon. There wouldn't be any place to stay in town, but they could ride on down the Grand and camp beside the river.

He'd see what Luke and Dolan said. The closer he came to the Big J, the more a sense of uneasiness grew in him. He wasn't sure why. He just had a hunch they ought to get off the Big J and the sooner the better.

Chapter XIX

JIM TURNBULL had breakfast in the hotel dining room. When he finished eating, he stepped into the lobby, ignoring Cold Dan Summers who sat at a table near the door. He paid his bill, and when the clerk asked if he was leaving town before the races, he said he'd go out to the track for an hour or so because he'd made some bets on horses that were running this morning, but he'd be leaving for Grand Junction about noon. He guessed he couldn't find a horse ranch around Hillcrest that suited him. He'd keep looking, though. He might find what he wanted around Delta or Montrose.

He climbed the stairs to his room, packed the few things he had brought with him, and left, carrying his Winchester in one hand and his haversack in the other. He had to make the same explanation to the stableman he had made to the hotel clerk, then he mounted and rode east out of town. Half an hour later he reined toward the river, dismounted under some cottonwoods and tied his horse. He stripped gear from the animal, found a grassy spot in the shade, and lay down, his head on his saddle.

Turnbull was never nervous during the actual holdup or the gunfight which often followed. For some reason he had always been nervous on the first day he spent in a community he planned to rob, and on the day of the robbery just before it happened. Now he lighted a cigar, and tried to picture the good, rich life that he'd have when he got to Mexico with a loaded money belt.

Somehow the mental picture of that good rich life just

wouldn't come. He finished his cigar and threw the stub into the river. He tried to doze, but he could not. Then, suddenly, he thought of Judy Dunn. He didn't want to think of her, but once she had popped into his mind, he couldn't get her out. He'd had a good time with the waitress from the hotel dining room in Hillcrest, but she knew how to put a man in his place. Judy hadn't.

Come to think of it, there had never been anything very exciting about Judy. She was just a big, strong country girl who had been as ignorant as a baby. She had welcomed his advances because she saw in him a chance to escape a home and community she hated. He took her with him because she was a woman. To Jim Turnbull a woman was a "thing," an "object," not anything to love and cherish, but something to own just as he owned his horse. For a time he had owned Judy Dunn.

He had reserved the right to rid himself of her when he was tired of her; he did not under any circumstances give her the right to leave him. But that was what she had done. Well, he'd settle with her before the day was over. She knew how he felt about anyone who deserted him. Now he would see that she paid.

He had stayed out of jail because he had never left anyone behind who could identify him. He wasn't starting now by leaving Judy. Apparently she hadn't talked, but who knew when she would change her mind and blab everything she knew about him. If, of course, she had regained her memory. He didn't believe she had lost it forever. That would be too much luck to count on.

He spent the rest of the morning until it was time to return to Hillcrest thinking how he would make her pay. Oddly enough, he found far more personal satisfaction thinking about Judy than he had in his day dream about Mexico. Maybe he would take her with him. There was no hurry about killing her. It was enough for her to know that sooner or later that was what would happen. The time would be his to choose.

He saddled up and rode back into Hillcrest, arriving in the business block before noon. Main Street was deserted exactly as he had expected. He heard the crowd at the race track give out a great cheer, and grinned. Let the suckers bet their money on horses. That wasn't for him.

Only a fool would bet on a horse race. He wanted a sure thing, like the money in Abe Runkel's safe.

Cold Dan Summers horse was racked in front of the store, but Summers wasn't in sight. The other four men were in the street, riding slowly toward the store. Turnbull was still half a block away when Summers ran out of the store, untied his horse, and swung up.

Summers saw Turnbull and motioned for him to come on. He dug in his spurs and rocketed out of town, heading north on the Banner Creek road. He motioned to the other men and they fell in behind him and kept the same, hard pace he was setting.

Turnbull reined up in the middle of the street, shocked into a sort of paralysis. He had no idea what had got into Summers; the man's crazy actions made no sense at all. Then the thought struck him that maybe Summers had held the store up by himself. Or maybe he'd tried and failed.

Turnbull felt a hot, consuming rage possess him as he cracked steel to his horse. If either notion turned out to be true, he'd kill the bastard when he caught him. Only one thing was certain. Summers had finally and completely ruined weeks of waiting and planning. They could not go back to the store now. Runkel would know what was in the air, or at least make a good guess. Summers must have given the scheme away or he wouldn't be leaving the way he had. Runkel would have the place filled with the sheriff and his deputies before Turnbull and his men could get back into town.

Summers was a mile from Hillcrest when he stopped and dismounted, the others reining in beside him. Turnbull was the last to arrive. He stepped down at once and faced Summers no more than thirty feet from him, his right hand close to the butt of his gun.

"Dan, I think I'm going to kill you," Turnbull said. "Just what in hell made you do a fool stunt like that? We can't go back now and you know it."

"Kill me?" Summers stared at him incredulously. "I save your worthless hide and you want to kill me. What kind of an idiot are you?"

Turnbull snorted in contempt. "Just how do you make out you saved my life? We were all there ready to move in. We were on time, but you jumped the gun. Did you try to clean out the safe by yourself?"

"No, I didn't," Summers snapped. "That store was full of armed men. They were hiding behind the counter just waiting for us to walk in. If we had, they'd have smoked us down. Or maybe we'd all have gone to the pen for twenty years." His lips curled in distaste and he spat into the dust in front of him. "I should have let 'em take you, I reckon."

Turnbull stared. That was all he could do. He just stood there beside his horse and stared at Summers, wondering if the man was lying. He decided Summers was telling the truth, but how had it happened? They had never been sold out before.

"How'd they get onto us?" Pete Keller demanded, his gaze pinned on Turnbull's face. "If you got drunk and done some bragging so help me, I'll shoot your eyes out."

"No, I didn't get drunk," Turnbull shouted angrily. "How would I know how they got onto us? Maybe one of you got drunk. Maybe one of you done the bragging."

"All I know is that they were ready for us," Summers said. "I feel like I'd just walked away from my own funeral."

"How'd you happen to go into the store?" Turnbull asked.

"Good luck, mostly," Summers answered. "I was in the hotel bar having a drink. I'd been sitting at a table just waiting for the time to go by. I got tired of sitting, so I walked to the batwings and looked into the street. That's where the luck came in. I was standing there about half past eleven when the fat sheriff led a bunch of men into the store.

"I went back to my table and sat down and thought about it for twenty minutes or so. I knowed something was wrong, but I couldn't see how the sheriff had got onto what we were up to. Finally I decided to find out for sure before I warned the rest of you. They might have gone into the store to pay off some bets. Anyhow, I went into the store and asked for a box of 45 shells.

"Nobody was in sight except the storekeeper. He was in the back beside the safe and he got excited when I came in.

He told me to get out and said the store wasn't open. I went right on to where he was standing and said I had to have shells. The old goat backed up and I went after him around the end of the counter. That was when I seen all these men squatting down back of the counter.

"One of 'em motioned with his gun for me to git and I done it pronto. I figured they might change their minds if they suspicioned who I was. They didn't. I guess they just took me for another cowhand who was in town for the races."

Turnbull was only half listening. When Summers finished talking, Turnbull said, "We've got to leave the country. We'll stop by the Big J on our way. I don't think that fat sheriff will get a posse after us, seeing as we didn't do nothing, but there's no sense in taking chances."

He mounted and rode up the creek, not waiting for anybody to argue with him. He'd stop at the Big J even if he did it alone. He hadn't gone fifty yards until he glanced back and saw that the others were strung out behind him.

He knew how Ed Drumm had been warned. Judy had talked. There could be no other explanation. Maybe she had talked a week or more ago and Drumm had waited, hoping to bag the whole outfit. He'd come close to doing it, too.

Turnbull had no way of knowing the time when Judy had informed on him, but it didn't make any difference. They had lost their chance and now he'd have to go to Cheyenne and plan the next job. They wouldn't pick up enough at the Big J to replace what they had just lost.

Let the rest of the gang guess how Drumm had been informed, Turnbull told himself. He couldn't risk telling them it was Judy and that he had known all the time where she was. They would have asked him why he hadn't shut her mouth for good. He'd failed once, but he could have kept trying until he succeeded. Instead he'd let it slide, thinking that she hadn't talked and therefore she wouldn't, or that she'd never regained her memory. Well, he'd been a careless idiot and there was no way getting around it.

No amount of self-condemnation helped. He'd just make sure that Judy didn't survive the robbery at the Big

J. Or any of the Jones family, either. He put his mind to the job of planning how to handle the four men who could all be home. Some of them, or all of them, might be in town for the races. That would make it easier, but it would mean waiting until evening when the Jones men returned.

Turnbull reached the side road that led up the mesa hill to the Big J and stopped. When the others reached him, he ignored their sour looks, knowing he could not afford an argument.

"Dan, take Pancho and Ed and ride up this road to the mesa," Turnbull said. "There's not much cover when you reach the top on this side of the buildings. Just ride in like you were visitors. If there's any trouble, fort up in the barn or corral. Dick and Pete will come with me. Give us an hour before you go up the hill. There's quite a bit of brush north of the buildings and an arroyo we can use to get close to the house. We'll climb to the mesa farther north and slip up on the back of the house. If you keep 'em busy in front, we'll get at 'em from the back and we'll have 'em where the hair's short before they know what's happening."

"Suppose we run into some of 'em on the range?" Summers asked. "There ain't much chance they'll all be in the house on a day like this."

"Shoot 'em," Turnbull said curtly. "We're sure not leaving any witnesses. We can't tell what we'll find till we get there. The house might be empty. If they're in town watching the races, it will be, but we only need one to tell us where the dinero is."

Summers nodded, then he said in a cold, brittle tone, "We've told you before and now I'm telling you once more. That dinero had better be there."

"It will be."

Turnbull jerked his head at Lucky Dick Norton and Pete Keller and rode up the creek.

Chapter XX

WHEN BUD reached the Big J after seeing Sheriff Ed Drumm in town, he found Judy waiting for him at the corral, her face troubled. He stepped down and asked, "What's wrong?"

"Nothing yet," she said. "Not anything more than was wrong yesterday."

He stripped gear from his horse, glancing at her white face, and said, "Something's wrong that wasn't wrong this morning, Judy. You'd better tell me what it is."

"Your pa saddled up and rode off a while ago," she said. "I thought you were never going to get back. Dolan's been sitting in the front room with his shotgun on his lap. He's been staring at your pa as if he wanted him to start a row. Luke walks back and forth like a nervous bear. You're the only one who can cool Dolan off."

Bud turned his horse into the corral and walked toward the house, Judy beside him. He said, "All the way home I kept thinking we ought to saddle up and get off the Big J before we have a blow up. I don't want to leave before we get Luke's and Dolan's wages from Pa, though, so I guess we'd better wait till he gets back."

"Don't go today," she cried passionately. "I tell you that Turnbull and his men, or some of them anyway, will be here this afternoon. I don't want to run into them on the road."

He reached the porch and stopped to look at the girl. She puzzled him. At times she still seemed to be holding back information. Dolan and Luke came out of the house,

Dolan carrying his shotgun, Luke so jittery he couldn't stand still. Bud had never seen him this jumpy before.

"You see Drumm?" Dolan demanded.

Bud nodded. "He'll take care of the store safe, all right, but I clean forgot to tell him that Judy thinks Turnbull will show up out here. I aimed to and thought he might ride out after the ruckus was over in the store. Of course if Ed and his deputies wipe Turnbull's gang out or jail them, they won't be here."

"That's not likely to happen," Judy said. "Turnbull and his men can smell trouble. They won't tackle the safe if the sheriff is there with some deputies."

Bud shot quick glances at Luke and then at Dolan, wondering if the girl had told them anything she hadn't told him. He brought his gaze to Judy's drawn face. He said, "I've got a hunch you haven't told us everything."

"Yes, I have," she said quickly. "I don't know anything else to tell you. I'm just afraid. That's all. I guess you'd call it woman's intuition, but I get a little more afraid each minute. I tell you I know they'll be here."

Her woman's intuition did not convince him. He asked, "Why would we be any better off here than if we met 'em on the road?"

She moistened dry, cracked lips with the tip of her tongue. "I . . . well, there's six of them. It seems to me you'd have a better chance holding them off if we were in the house." She cleared her throat, then cried out, "Bud, have you ever met a man who would kill somebody because he enjoyed doing it?"

"No."

"Then you don't know what Jim Turnbull is like."

Judy was in no condition to ride this afternoon. She might become hysterical if he forced her to, he thought. It was plain, then, that they could not leave until morning. The danger of a blow up between Dolan and his father would continue for another fifteen or twenty hours.

"All right," Bud said. "We'll leave early in the morning. Go get dinner, Judy. My tape worm's beginning to holler."

She nodded and hurried into the house. "How about it, Dolan?" Bud asked. "You have any trouble with Pa?"

"No," Dolan said in a belligerent tone, "but I was ready for it."

"That's right," Luke said glumly. "I'm glad you're back, Bud. Maybe you can pound some sense into him." He threw out a hand toward Dolan. "Sometimes I get a notion I don't know him. I think he's a little crazy."

"You bet I am," Dolan snapped. "I'm as crazy as a hoot owl, crazy enough not to take anything more off Pa. I'm damned if I know why you've put up with Pa all these years."

"Neither do I," Luke admitted.

"Judy and me are getting married as soon as we get to town," Dolan said. "I'll find some kind of a job, even if it's only sweeping out a saloon. I was holding back, figuring I had to prove I could take care of her, but I ain't holding back no more."

"You're sure, Dolan?" Bud asked. "She told you about her and Turnbull. It don't make no difference?"

"Not a damn bit," Dolan said, bristling. "Don't you say a word about what she was. It's what she is and what she's gonna be that counts."

"It's up to you," Bud said. "Just one thing. When Pa gets back, let me handle him. All I want is for us to get out of here without any of us doing something we'll be sorry about afterwards."

Dolan nodded agreement. "That's jake with me. The truth is I've been afraid of what I'd do if he gets ornery again."

It was late in the afternoon when Adam rode back into the yard and reined up in front of the house. He stepped down and, leaving his horse tied to the hitch rail, strode into the house carrying a gunnysack. He dropped the sack on the oak stand, his gaze moving from Luke to Bud to Dolan who still carried the shotgun. Beads of sweat formed on his forehead and cheeks and dribbled down to his chin. He wiped a sleeve across his face, ignoring Judy who had come into the room from the kitchen.

"You want your dinner now, Mr. Jones?" Judy asked.

Adam still ignored her. His pulse was pounding in his temples. He was tired, Bud thought, and nervous and cranky, but the part that amazed Bud the most was the fact that Adam Jones was beaten. He had felt it before; now he felt it more strongly than ever. This was incredible because he had always believed that his father was a man who could not be whipped by anything or anyone.

"I don't trust banks," Adam said. "You know that, but you likely thought I had my savings hid around the house. It ain't important where they was, but it was a long ways from here. I figured that someday we'd have visitors who thought they could find it somewhere around the house. Here it is, every cent we've saved and worked for since your ma left us."

Adam patted the sack. "Right now with you boys fixing to leave me, I'm wondering why I scrimped and saved like I have. I don't even know for sure what I would have done with the money if we'd gone on like we always had, but now I've got a proposition to make to you."

He emptied the sack on the oak stand. Bud stared in shocked surprise. He had never seen more than a few dollars at any one time in his life, but here were at least fifteen canvas sacks bulging with coins and greenbacks. Adam smiled a little, the first time Bud had seen him smile since he had offered to marry Judy.

"There's a little over twelve thousand dollars in them sacks," he said. "All this time I thought I was doing right raising you boys the way I done. I wanted to make you tough enough to stand anything that happened to you." He looked at Dolan. "Don't get sore, boy, but I've got to say this. I wanted you to be tough enough to stand having a woman you love run off with another man. I wasn't."

"Judy won't ever do that," Dolan grated. "By God, she won't."

"We'll see, we'll see," Adam said. "Now here's my proposition. If you're still bound to pull out, I'll pay Luke and Dolan what they've got coming in wages, but if you two will stay, we'll split this dinero three ways which means $4,000 for each of you."

He pinned his gaze on Dolan's face. "You get your share, too, but I don't want you around here. Take your woman and the money and git. I never found out what the hell you're good for anyway. Luke and Bud are the ones I want." He looked at Luke, then Bud, hesitated, and added, "You can do what you want to with your share. All I ask is that you stay here and work the outfit. We'll get a woman to keep house, too. Think it over while I put my horse away."

He wheeled and stomped out of the house. Bud said softly, "Well, what do you know about that?"

"I'll be glad to take my share and git," Dolan said harshly. "We'll make out fine, me'n Judy. I ain't good for nothin' the way Pa sees it and that's a fact."

"Sure we'll make out," Judy added.

Luke walked to the oak stand and stood staring at the money. He felt of one of the sacks and shook his head. "I dunno, Bud. I don't know what to say."

"Bud." Judy had gone to the front door. "They're out there at the corral. Three of them with your Pa. We were so interested in him we forgot to watch."

Bud ran to the front door. Three men were standing beside the horse trough near the corral. Adam had put his horse through the gate into the corral and shut it, then turned to the men and said something.

"Get him in here," Judy whispered. "They'll kill him."

"Naw, Pa can take all three of 'em if it comes to a fight," Luke said.

"Is one of 'em Turnbull?" Bud asked.

"No," Judy answered.

"I'm going out there," Bud said, "in case they start anything. Judy, go into the kitchen. It'll be safer in there."

"Maybe these men ain't part of Turnbull's outfit," Dolan said.

"Yes, they are," Judy said. "I don't know their names, but I've seen them. Don't go out there, Bud."

"Go into the kitchen, I told you," he said, and this time she obeyed.

He stepped through the door and onto the porch, his eyes on his father. He was not as sure as Luke was that Adam could handle the three outlaws. Then it happened, so fast he was stunned. Adam reached for his Colt, but he never got it out of leather. The man closest to him drew his Colt, a fast, smooth draw, and shot Adam, the report slamming into the afternoon quiet. Adam staggered and sprawled into the dust near the trough as the three outlaws dived behind it.

For an instant Bud stood rooted on the porch until Dolan yelled, "Get inside."

The men behind the horse trough started firing, one bullet splintering a porch post within inches of Bud's head. He whirled and dived inside as Luke and Dolan answered the outlaws' fire. He slammed the door shut and dropped the bar, then fell belly flat to the floor. When he glanced toward the kitchen, he saw that Judy had come back into the front room again.

"You get into the kitchen and you stay there," Bud yelled.

She retreated through the doorway. For a short time Bud watched Luke and Dolan at the windows, firing and dropping down and levering shells into the chambers again and firing. Bullets ripped through the shattered glass in the windows and through the front of the house to scream across the room and bury themselves into the far wall.

Dolan had laid his shotgun down and had grabbed the second rifle off the antler rack. There were only the two Winchesters in the house and Bud saw no sense in adding his six-shooter to the rifles. He'd have to get closer for his .45 to be effective and he knew how he could do it.

"Keep 'em busy," he shouted above the crackle of rifle fire. "I'm going to root 'em out from behind that horse trough."

He had crawled halfway across the front room to the kitchen door when he heard Judy scream. He guessed what had happened and cursed himself for not barring the back door.

"Dolan, get your scattergun," he shouted as he drew his revolver from the holster.

Bud came up from the floor and lunged through the doorway into the kitchen. He glimpsed Judy struggling in the arms of a big man. Two more men stood just inside the back door. The instant he cleared the door, Judy tipped her head and bit the big man's arm. He yelled and slackened his grip enough for her to free one arm. He held his six-shooter in his right hand. Now he threw a quick shot at Bud, but Judy jiggled his arm enough to make him miss.

Bud fired, taking the closest of the two outlaws near the back door, his bullet striking the man in the nose and angling upward through his brain. The third man had time for one shot at Bud. The slug drew blood, gouging out a furrow in the flesh along Bud's ribs on his right side. It was the only shot he fired. Bud's second bullet caught him in the chest. He stumbled back against the wall near the cookstove, his feet slid out from under him and he went down, his mouth springing open as his head tipped forward on his chest.

The situation had forced Bud to make a lightning decision. He had purposely left the big man to Judy and Dolan, thinking that the outlaw would not have a chance to shoot straight as he struggled with Judy. Now, turning toward them, he heard the boom of the shotgun.

Dolan wasn't more than ten feet from the man, smoke still drifting from the muzzle of the shotgun when Bud turned. Judy had fought herself free and had dropped to the floor only seconds before Dolan let go with the shotgun. The buckshot ripped off much of the top of the big man's skull.

"Tell Luke to keep shooting," Bud said.

He raced out through the door and across the porch and around the woodshed, then the privy, and finally a small log cabin that had been Adam's first home on the Big J and was now used as a tool shed. When Bud cleared the cabin, he had made more than a half circle after leaving the house, so now the horse trough was no longer any protection for the three outlaws who had forted up behind it. Bud had a clear shot at them, but he missed. It served as a warning to them that their position had changed. They scurried around the corral toward their horses, wanting no part of the fight now.

Bud nailed one of the men before he reached his horse, sending him into a stumbling fall. He went to the ground and rolled over, then getting up on his knees, fired once, the bullet ripping through the sleeve of Bud's shirt. Bud used the last bullet in his gun, knocking the man over. Judging from the way he fell, he was finished.

Stepping behind the cabin, Bud reloaded, and when he moved back to see where the outlaws had gone, he heard Luke's great yell of triumph and saw that the remaining two bandits were on their horses and cracking steel to the animals as they raced southward.

Bud raised his revolver to fire at them, then lowered it. They were moving too fast. He would have no chance of hitting one of them. He holstered his gun and, running to the corral, looked at the man he had shot. He was dead, and Bud, glancing at his face, saw that he was the man who had shot Adam.

Luke and Dolan left the house and ran to where their father lay. When Bud joined them, he saw that Adam was still alive, but death was only seconds away. He knelt beside his father, Luke on the other side.

"It's your now," Adam whispered. "All the money and the Big J. Stay and work it. Promise?"

"We promise," Luke said.

"Sure," Bud said. "We promise."

Slowly Adam turned his eyes to Dolan who stood at his feet looking down at him. He tried to say something, but his strength was gone. A moment later he was dead.

Bud rose. He looked at the house, at Judy who stood watching them from the porch, and thought that everything had happened so fast in these last few minutes that he could not fully grasp the significance of these events, but one thought crowded out the others. A little while ago he and his brothers had wanted to get away from their father, but now he was the one who had left them.

Dolan ran toward Judy as Luke dropped a hand on Bud's shoulder. He said, "Partners?"

Bud nodded. "Partners," he said.

THE END

Wayne D. Overholser has won three Golden Spur awards from the Western Writers of America and has a long list of fine Western titles to his credit. He was born in Pomeroy, Washington, and attended the University of Montana, University of Oregon, and the University of Southern California before becoming a public school teacher and principal in various Oregon communities. He began writing for Western pulp magazines in 1936 and within a couple of years was a regular contributor to Street & Smith's *Western Story* and Fiction House's *Lariat Story Magazine*. *Buckaroo's Code* (1948) was his first Western novel and remains one of his best. In the 1950s and 1960s, having retired from academic work to concentrate on writing, he would publish as many as four books a year under his own name or a pseudonym, most prominently as Joseph Wayne. *The Bitter Night, The Lone Deputy,* and *The Violent Land* are among the finest of the early Overholser titles. He was asked by William MacLeod Raine, that dean among Western writers, to complete his last novel after Raine's death. Some of Overholser's most rewarding novels were actually collaborations with other Western writers: *Colorado Gold* with Chad Merriman and *Showdown at Stony Creek* with Lewis B. Patten. Overholser's Western novels, no matter under what name they have been published, are based on a solid knowledge of the history and customs of the American frontier West, particularly when set in his two favorite Western states, Oregon and Colorado. When it comes to his characters, he writes with skill, an uncommon sensitivity, and a consistently vivid and accurate vision of a way of life unique in human history.